Other books by Lee Gutkind:

BIKE FEVER
THE BEST SEAT IN BASEBALL, BUT YOU HAVE TO STAND!

and the film
A PLACE JUST RIGHT

GOD'S HELICOPTER

GOD'S HELICOPTER

Lee Gutkind

To Linda —
Lee Gutkind

SLOW LORIS PRESS
Pittsburgh

Sections of this novel originally appeared in *Slow Loris Reader*.

The writer gratefully acknowledges the National Endowment of the Arts for financial support while writing, and the Virginia Center for the Creative Arts, where parts of this book were written.

Printed in the United States of America
Hoechstetter Printing Company
Pittsburgh, Pennsylvania

Library of Congress Cataloging in Publication Data

Gutkind, Lee.
  God's helicopter.

  I. Title.
PS3557.U88G6   1982   813'.54   82-19533
ISBN 0-918366-26-7

Published by SLOW LORIS PRESS
923 Highview Street
Pittsburgh, Pennsylvania 15206

To my friend and teacher, Montgomery Culver

Chapter I

Middlebaum's Doom

It happened the night Willie's ulcer launched a surprise attack on his stomach.

Willie staggered into the bathroom, dropped his pajama bottoms and sat down on the cold toilet seat, twisting and shivering, rocking back and forth in painful rhythm, biting into the knuckles of his fist until blood mixed with saliva rushed into his mouth and down his throat, tasting flat like metal.

He fell forward and rolled over, beating his feet against the wall, attempting to shift the pain from one place to another, struggling to free himself of the pajama bottoms caught between his feet and crotch. His mother came immediately, although hours of fire and hell seemed to pass before she switched on the light and found him crumpled there, blinking at the sudden explosion of yellow. He felt her pulling his pajamas away, liberating him. He listened to how soft her voice was, the softest he had ever heard it, how she comforted him, saying it would be OK, all right, not to worry, if he swallowed the medicine and went to sleep. Her arm was a warm electric pillow on his back as she guided him out of the bathroom and into the living room. Then he was on the couch and the smooth cool quilt came up over his stomach, caressing him to the neck. He washed down a pill with warm milk, thick and sweet, gagged and dripped some on the pillows. But she said she didn't care, just to drink slowly as she wiped his fist dry, painted his knuckles with Mercurochrome, took a warm washcloth and caressed his feet, legs, stomach, his sticky mouth. Pretty soon, maybe hours and maybe minutes later, all he could feel was the quilt being tucked under his heels and his feet tingling cool and clean after being wiped and washed in the warm water.

It was 1955, and for his whole life—twelve years—Willie Heinemann lived in Pittsburgh with his ulcer. It was fall, Ike was President, the leaves were changing colors and complexions, and Ralph Kiner, left fielder for the Pittsburgh Pirates, was the greatest man ever to live.

Lying there, Willie was conscious of his parents talking, though he did not try to listen; he was just there, thinking of nothing, basking in the aura of relief from pain. Eventually, he became aware of the conversation, although the voices seemed to be coming from a radio turned very low, from wires strung out for thousands of miles, losing treble and pitch at every little town along the way, transmitting words that sounded hollow, vapory, ghost-like.

"We're lucky," his mother was saying, "Willie will get better."

"The doctor *says* Willie will get better," said Harry Heinemann, and Willie could hear him move in his bed, the wooden floor creaking with the shifting of his weight.

"If you can't believe the doctor, who can you believe?" Sarah said. "Willie will get better, it's not serious. He's got to keep taking pills, drinking milk, and he's got to stop worrying about everything. He thinks too much, that's what the doctor says. Kids should have fun, shouldn't be thinking all the time. But Ronald is different. The doctor told Ruth he'd only get worse."

Ronald? Who was Ronald?

"It's spreading," Sarah was saying.

"I thought the last operation cut out the malignancy."

Malignancy is cancer. What are they talking about? Who is Ronald? Why don't they shut up so I can sleep?

"Ruth says they thought they could stop the growth, but it didn't work. It was a chance. The poor kid, he doesn't know."

"He doesn't know anything?"

"Not about the malignancy, or even why he had an operation. They told him it was for asthma."

"Does he have asthma?"

"He's got everything else, what would stop him from having asthma?"

"But doesn't he have asthma?"

"They just told him that when they discovered what he really had."

Ruth, Willie thought, *Ruth Middlebaum*, his mother's friend. So it is her son, Ronald Middlebaum, who is getting worse, who has the cancer and malignancy all over his body. Ronald Middlebaum, who used to visit on Saturdays with his mother to play games and build buildings with alphabet building blocks.

"I really don't know what to tell Ruth. I mean, she's such a nice person, and it's going to be so hard for her to face what's going to happen. He's going to die."

"You have to sympathize," said Harry Heinemann. "That's all, there's nothing you can do. You can't stop it, there's just nothing else to do but sympathize."

Cancer, something that grows and grows in your body. Also a constellation. Willie learned it from Miss Schlegel's science class, fifth period of the fourth grade.

"But what can I say?"

"You can't say anything. She knows you feel bad. You can't say, 'I'm sorry your son might die,' and expect to cheer her up. Just listen to her and be nice. And thank God that our son has nothing more wrong with him than an ulcer from a nervous condition."

"It isn't fair," said Sarah.

"Don't be silly. Fair has nothing to do with it. How long till the kid gets really bad?"

"The doctor isn't sure, maybe six months. Then Ruth doesn't know what's going to be. She says they might try another operation, but probably nothing will help. God, it's awful."

Willie kept listening, but eventually lost the words to the gray empty fog that preceded all his dreams. He thought about Middlebaum, while the voices in the other room grew more distant. Soon, Willie could see those miles of radio wire, strung out over the corn and desert and tumbleweed. He could even see the sound carried by the wires, moving like a distant locomotive, never stopping or wavering, changing speed or direction, sound coming from an infinite double line of wire, taut and straight, continuing forever, a ceaseless vehicle that climbed toward the clouds, but never quite reached the sky.

Once Willie heard his father tell a joke about syphilis. Willie knew what "The Syph" was, of course, but didn't quite understand the joke. Two Negro soldiers went into a whorehouse and, after they came out, a friend came up and said that those whores had syphilis. But the two Negroes didn't know what "The Syph" was, so they went to the doctor and said: "Doctor, what is syphilis?" And the doctor said: "Boys, syphilis is a disease of the privates." Then the two Negro soldiers smiled, and the way his father told it, Willie could see teeth flashing white against midnight faces. "Then we ain't got nuthin' to worry 'bout, Doc," said the two soldiers, " 'cause we is sergeants."

That was all Willie could remember. And as the train of sleep clattered through the tunnel of his mind, Willie dreamed of having Ronald Middlebaum promoted to sergeant, because cancer was for privates, and from it, sergeants never die. Willie dreamed. He dreamed and dreamed.

Willie and Middlebaum were building Abe Lincoln's log cabin. Willie was Honest Abe and Middlebaum was Honest Abe's father, and Abe was telling his father about all the books he was reading by the firelight at night.

"I read the Bible," said Abe, tugging on his beard and tipping his stovepipe hat. "I memorized the first twelve chapters. I read *Gone With the Wind* four times, but I never read comic books. Comic books are bad for your eyes."

"And what else have you done, my son?" said Honest Abe's father, nodding with approval.

"I chopped firewood for the winter. I built a fence a mile long. I fed the chickens and put two coats of paint on the barn."

"You're a good boy, my son."

"Someday I'm going to be President of the United States and free the slaves in the South."

Willie and Middlebaum were Abraham and Joseph. Willie wore his father's terrycloth bathrobe of many colors, and Willie was asking Middlebaum, who was playing Abraham, about there being only one God and why he couldn't meet Him, and Abraham was describing his vision, his communication with this one God, and how He told him that the Jews were the chosen people, chosen to carry His words across Canaan and Egypt and Palestine and Rome, telling everyone to destroy their idols and worship the one God alone.

"But why can't I meet this one God?" said Joseph, wrapping the bathrobe of many colors around his slender frame, leaning on a broom that had suddenly become a staff. "Why isn't He making any personal appearances?"

"Because, my son," said Abraham, nodding his head and puffing on a pipe that was a pencil, "half of the world is in darkness and the other half is in light."

"I don't understand, father."

"God presides each day over the lighted side of the world, my son, and God is too busy with all of His businesses and duties to meet anyone, except for me, His prophet, and the wisest man on earth."

Willie tossed and turned in his bed. Even in sleep his body could not be quiet. The pictures in his mind came and went, as the dream train chugged deeper into him.

Willie and Middlebaum were chopping down the cherry tree and throwing tea into the bay in Boston, fighting the red coats with Paul Revere, hiding in the mountains with Judah Maccabee, hearing God's words come from the burning bush that looked like a radiator. They were Otto Graham throwing touchdown passes, Lou Groza kicking field goals, Ralph Kiner hitting homeruns. They were the Lone Ranger and Tonto, Hopalong Cassidy and Lucky, Roy Rogers and Gabby Hayes, bringing truth and justice and the American way of life to the lawless western prairie.

After they had been in school for a while, Middlebaum and Willie slowly drifted apart. Soon they were no longer friends. Willie noticed, however, that Middlebaum would suddenly disappear from school for weeks at a time and come back looking hungry, his skin stretched tight like elastic against his face.

One afternoon, Middlebaum was found in the bathroom, coughing, choking, slobbering on the cold, vile floor. Willie watched as two white-coated attendants carried Middlebaum on a stretcher to an ambulance waiting outside. Somebody found out later that Middlebaum had scarlet fever, but Willie distinctly remembered that Middlebaum's face was white as chalk.

The years passed, second, third, fourth grades, Miss Schmeltz, Miss Schlegel, Miss Schwartz. Willie remembered how in school

Middlebaum often couldn't answer any of the teacher's questions, Middlebaum taking what seemed like an hour to read a sentence out loud, Middlebaum unable to work arithmetic problems on the blackboard. Middlebaum with thumbtacks on his chair, egg in his hair; Middlebaum being punched and tripped, the brunt of all the jokes. Willie got his licks in, too.

One day after school, Willie found himself walking down the street a few steps behind Melvin Zeewee and Bobby Kenner. He was in a hurry and wanted to pass, but decided to bide his time and show proper respect. After all, Kenner was the best homerun hitter at the school playground, while Zeewee was the meanest, toughest kid in school. Both Zeewee and Kenner were also full-fledged Greenfield kids.

One of Willie's biggest problems was that he did not come from Greenfield, the neighborhood down by the river where all of the kids whose fathers worked at the steel mills lived. One of Willie's other problems was that he did not live in Squirrel Hill, either, where all the rich doctors, lawyers and shoe store owners had their homes. The houses in Squirrel Hill had long driveways, big back yards and clean bricks. The houses in Greenfield were built Siamese-style and in rows charred with a century of dust and soot. The kids from Squirrel Hill dressed in madras shirts, pants with buckles on the back and hardly ever talked to the kids from Greenfield who wore bluejeans, played softball with ratty mitts and beat the hell out of a Squirrel Hill kid at least once a day for fun.

Everyone beat up Ronald Middlebaum, however, no matter where they lived.

That day, Willie remembered, Middlebaum had come up behind Willie, passing hurriedly, without a word. He was obviously very upset. His face was red, and under the flush of red there were scratches and smudges of dirt. Middlebaum tried walking by, but Zeewee moved in front of him, blocking his way. Middlebaum tried going around, but Zeewee caught the boy by the arm.

"What's your hurry? Don't you like us? Don't you want to talk to us?"

Middlebaum was silent. He had stopped obediently, but now started to tremble, lips quivering, nose twitching, cheeks quaking like leaves in a biting breeze.

"What happened to you, Middlebaum?" said Zeewee. "Where you been?"

14

Middlebaum, tall and rubbery, a pale splinter of a boy, his shoulders seeming no wider than his head, could not speak. He couldn't even look Zeewee in the eye. He kept turning away, trying to run, but Zeewee held tight.

"Somebody beat you up, didn't they?" Zeewee was acting very tough, talking out of the side of his mouth like a private eye in a movie.

"We asked you what happened, and when we ask you something, we want an answer," Kenner said.

Zeewee grabbed Middlebaum by the neck, pulled him close, then slammed him up against a tree. Zeewee and Kenner both were built solidly; not tall, but broad and barrel-like, nailed to the ground.

There was a ping pong ball in Middlebaum's throat. It bobbed up and down. "A couple of kids tripped me. I fell. They wouldn't let me get up." His voice was thin, pale and fragile like his face.

"That's just what we're going to do," Zeewee threatened.

"We might never let you go," said Kenner. "You'll be nailed to this tree for life."

Middlebaum struggled, but Zeewee's hand was a vise at his neck. "C'mon, let me go."

Fear flashed in Middlebaum's somber, raisin eyes, as he turned to Willie who was quietly watching. "Make them let me go, Willie."

Zeewee looked Willie up and down with a sneer. "Well now, Willie, are you gonna try to make us let him go?"

"You a friend of his or something?" Kenner asked, holding up the square hammer of his fist.

Willie just stood there, not knowing what to do, but fully aware that something had to be done; he didn't want to be put in the position of helping Middlebaum—especially in public. Zeewee and Kenner might find out about him once being Middlebaum's friend. On the other hand, he felt bad, didn't want to see the boy get hurt.

"Well, Willie," Zeewee said, "you gonna make us or not?" Zeewee began punching the palm of his left hand with the fist of his right, waiting for Willie to decide.

Suddenly, Willie stooped down, grabbed a stone, and hurled it at Middlebaum, hitting him in the knee. "You're a freak, Middlebaum," Willie yelled, "a freak!"

Zeewee paused to consider, then slammed Middlebaum against the tree once more for good measure. "Freak!" he yelled, stooping to gather up his own stones to throw.

Sprawled on the sidewalk, Middlebaum looked around in fear and confusion. When the stones came zinging by, he got to his feet almost reluctantly, and ran down the street, managing to stay ahead of most of the stones, and the voices calling him a freak, a freak.

"Middlebaum the freak!"

Chapter II
Shadowing Middlebaum

When Willie saw Middlebaum walking toward school that morning, he ducked behind the row of bushes that rimmed Herbert Hoover Grade School. Middlebaum bounced when he walked on shoes that seemingly had springs for soles, he went up so high with each step, and Willie wondered how a person with only six months to live could look so happy. If I were about to die, I'd make my parents give me lots of money, or I'd rob a bank and go to Paris or Detroit on a final fling. That's what I would do, rather than go to school, day-after-day, where everyone torments and teases me.

There was a chance, of course, that Willie's parents could be wrong about Middlebaum dying, but older people hardly ever joke about death because they are so close to it themselves. If Sarah and Harry were convinced that Middlebaum was going to die, there could be no doubt. Middlebaum had had it. But was Middlebaum aware of his fate? Could Middlebaum feel his blood turning to water, his heart beating slower, his brain evaporating? God usually warns people of upcoming death by wrinkling up their faces, graying their hair, depositing big brown blotches on their skin.

"Soon I won't be around anymore," Willie's grandparents, aunts, uncles would sometimes say. Or, "I'm coming to the end of the line. My time is almost up." And, more often than not, they were right. Willie's grandparents, relatives and their friends seemed to be dropping off at an alarming rate. Their main social activity was attending funerals—either as visitors or victims. Had Middlebaum gotten the word that he was next?

Through the rest of the day, Willie followed Middlebaum, watching him in classes, trailing him to the bathroom and water fountain, studying him carefully for tell-tale signs of death.

Middlebaum's hair was brown, his skin smooth and white as the ceiling. There were no pouches under his eyes, no limp in his leg; his fingers weren't gnarled like claws. But perhaps cancer sent out different warnings. Perhaps people dying from cancer bounce and whistle when they walk, and a ping pong ball suddenly pops up in their throats. The ping pong ball grows bigger and bigger, day-after-day, till it finally chokes them to death.

After school, Willie hunched down behind the bushes and waited until Middlebaum passed by, then followed him down Murray Avenue and over the Beechwood Boulevard Bridge. This hulking arch, splotched black and gray with soot from the mills, served as a dividing line between the best and the worst of the families whose children attended Herbert Hoover. Greenfield, where the bad kids lived, was on one side of the bridge, its outskirts beginning two blocks down toward the slag piles and the muddy slab known as the Monongahela River. Squirrel Hill, with its velvet lawns, glittering Cadillacs and sculptured shrubs, where all the men over 21-years-of-age wore diamond rings on their pinky fingers, began two blocks up from the bridge in the other direction.

Although Middlebaum lived closer to Greenfield, and Willie nearer Squirrel Hill, both were stuck in the middle, clustered like ants on a hill in a four-block area surrounding the bridge, a no-man's land of houses and streets, with no attachments, except to the bridge, and no synagogues, churches, cemeteries, parks, grocery stores and, worst of all, no name.

When asked where he lived, Willie would sometimes spit hockers, stuff his hands into his pockets and mumble out of the side of his mouth that Greenfield was his home. Other times, especially when talking with older people, Willie would pretend he was from Squirrel Hill, to impress them with his father's nonexistent wealth. He knew he wasn't fooling anyone; however, where he lived bothered him terribly. It bothered him not to be able to say for sure he was from one place or another. For his whole career at Herbert Hoover Grade School, Willie had wandered aimlessly from group-to-group, place-to-place, unable or perhaps unwilling to catch on, cursed with the fate of living in a neighborhood so unworthy as to not have a name.

Derban, Middlebaum's street, was very narrow, with cars parked on both sides, leaving only a single thru-lane for traffic. Like the street, the houses were small and narrow, yards cluttered with bushes, hoses, sprinklers, canvas swimming pools and patches of frail, hungry flowers.

Willie walked back and forth past Middlebaum's house. First, he went by quickly, head bent, as if on an important errand. In a while, he passed again, casually now, on a leisurely stroll. The third time, he crossed to the other side of the street, got down on his hands and knees and crawled from bush-to-bush, until he was directly opposite the house, on his stomach.

No one was on the porch. Everything was quiet, but the door was open and, through the screen, Willie could see a lounge chair, a table, a vase, a television flickering. He watched for a long time, waiting for someone to walk past the door, or come outside to hose down the sidewalk, or sit and rock on the glider. But nobody came; no movement, no sound.

The house, painted gray a long time ago, was now chipping. Underneath the layer of gray, Willie could make out a previous layer of gray paint, also chipping. And underneath the second, was surely a third layer of gray, and a fourth, as if the whole house had been put together with layers of drab gray paint.

For quite a while, Willie lay on the moist cool grass, his chin propped on his palm, staring across the street at Middlebaum's house, thinking quietly, picturing Middlebaum inside. At some point, he detected the odor of cooking cabbage, wafting like poison gas onto the street. He hated that smell. It reminded him of rubbish and dog shit and decaying dead rats.

Willie buried his nose in the grass and sucked in the air of the earth. He grabbed a flower and blanketed his nose with a blossom, pressed a handful of leaves against his mouth, but still couldn't camouflage the awful smell of the cooking cabbage. It hit him then that the cabbage was as close as he had ever come to actually knowing the odor of upcoming death. The cabbage had him captured, just as death had captured Ronald Middlebaum, and no matter how hard Willie tried, he was unable to purge the smell of death that came with the cabbage. There was no escape.

A person could not die and then get up the next day and walk to school. A person could not get a penicillin shot from Dr. Goldfield and kill the death. A person could not have an operation or go away on a long vacation or worship at the synagogue to cure or cleanse away the death. Willie had gone to his grandfather's funeral, and he had never seen his grandfather again. One down, three to go. He had watched some of his grandfather's relatives and friends come over to the house to visit, nice people who were plump and jolly and gave him nickels and dimes, "flavored by the U.S. Mint." Then they had died, and there were no more nickels, no more dimes, no more visits, no more mints. They never came back. They were dead. Dead is forever. Dead is dead. Dead was what was going to happen to Ronald Middlebaum.

Willie's whole body shook as he finally struggled to his feet and started to run. Away from Derban, down Lilac to Beechwood, Willie staggered and weaved, not from any serious affliction, but simply from shock. At twelve years old, at Middlebaum's age, it is impossible to die. Even if Middlebaum wanted to, he couldn't die. Death was for men with beards, for grandparents, for old ladies who wore hats. Those were the people who qualified.

* * *

Willie was an undercover agent, a counterspy for the good old F.B. of I., assigned to shadow Middlebaum. Willie spent the next few weeks hunting around the school, the halls, the bathroom, the playground, and then hiding from Middlebaum when he found him, watching closely, studying how Middlebaum walked and talked, what he was doing, finding out whom he played with, when he laughed, when he cried. All the while, Willie was searching carefully, examining the boy's profile, front view, back view, below and above, looking for signs of impending death. Then Willie reported his findings to J. Edgar Hoover or General MacArthur, personally.

Willie discovered that hardly anyone played with Middlebaum. Kids constantly ganged-up on him, stealing his Pittsburgh Pirate baseball cap, knocking his books out of his hands, into the mud. Middlebaum's shoulder was the school punching bag. Most days, he ran a gauntlet of Greenfield kids just to get home.

"Hey, Middlebaum, wanna fight?"

"Hey, pimple-head."

"Here comes niggy-nose."

"Take that," (KABOOM), "and that," (POW).

Middlebaum never fought back, accepting the harassment with a minimum of trembling and a resigned nonchalance. He was such a willing and tempting target that even Willie could hardly stifle the urge to jump out of concealment, run up and sock him himself.

Willie soon put together a list of Middlebaum's main activities for his superiors back at the Pentagon. Weekends, Middlebaum often crept into the woods behind Mrs. Glaze's house and set a small area of brush and weeds on fire. When the flames were going good, Middlebaum climbed to the roof of a nearby garage, spread out his arms and impersonated an airplane, RRRRRRRRRAAAAAAA, circling above. Then he picked up an axe that looked like a stick and parachuted into the thick of it, a brave and fearless forest ranger assigned to put out the blaze.

Sometimes he taunted Mrs. Crowley's boxer dog chained to a pole behind her house. Middlebaum would get as close to the dog as possible without its being able to bite him, so close to those urine-colored teeth he could feel the warmth and wetness of its angry breath. The dog would foam and growl, stretching in vain to get to Middlebaum's throat. Middlebaum often pretended that the boxer dog, drooling spittle, was really a Nazi sentry, and that he himself, Captain Middlebaum, was a commando assigned to knock out the German position with grenades resembling stones. Then he'd hide behind a bunker that looked like a bush, jump up and charge the dog, rocks flying, yelling authentic German words like "Heil Hitler," "Wiener schnitzel" and "fucker-oonie."

After school most days, Middlebaum worked hard on his homework, sitting on his front porch, hunching his broomstick body over a table, writing in his looseleaf notebook, scrambling through pages of text, not once ever looking up or taking breaks for glasses of Coke or anonymous telephone calls.

Every now and then, Middlebaum went to Shirley Millmaker's house and peeked into her bedroom window to watch her comb her hair. Or, he went over to eight-year-old Richard Kolkett's house, to break his toys and beat him up. Lenny Bernstein, who played the tuba for the Pitt band, lived farther down the street, and Middlebaum would often stop to say hello and drink a glass of water. Once, Willie watched Middlebaum pour the water into the mouth of the tuba when Lenny wasn't looking. And almost every evening around dinner-time, Middlebaum hid in the bushes under the Tanner's kitchen window and listened, while Mr. and Mrs. Tanner argued their way to divorce.

Middlebaum's only friend was Shepard Silver, a slight, short boy with thick black hair falling over his forehead, horn-rimmed spectacles, and freckled cheeks. Most people called him "Rip," not because he was tough and mean and went around ripping people apart with his bare hands, but because he owned a genuine Pittsburgh Pirate baseball jacket with a "rip" in one of the sleeves. The jacket had been actually worn by someone on the team, Rip claimed, maybe even Ralph Kiner himself. It had been found by Rip's father in a rubbish heap outside the stadium. Rip's father was a "huckster," who went around the city in his pick-up truck, selling vegetables and collecting junk. Rip told everybody his dad was a traveling salesman.

What Rip Silver had in common with Ronald Middlebaum, Willie couldn't at all imagine. Rip was the smartest kid in school; Willie suspected Rip built rockets in his basement, corresponded with President Eisenhower, and was already being begged by Harvard and Pitt to quit Herbert Hoover Grade School and become a professor. Rip was also very proper and mannerly, according to all the teachers. He brushed his teeth after every meal, shampooed his hair each night before he went to bed, and carried a clean handkerchief in his front pants pocket, no matter where he went.

Hunching under bushes, peering around corners, Willie watched when Middlebaum and Rip were together, gesturing and talking, laughing, throwing stones at fire hydrants. Willie strained his ears, even pulled them open wider, but never could he pull them open wide enough to hear what they were saying from so far away. How strange, Willie thought, as he slipped from house to bush to telephone pole, how you acquire reputations, establish yourself as being one thing or another, and how those impressions stick. Willie had called Middlebaum a freak, and to everyone, except maybe Rip, Middlebaum *was* a freak, would always be a freak and, within a matter of months, would undoubtedly be a dead freak. Middlebaum was a freak, Rip was a brain, Zeewee was tough.

And Willie? He was a nobody with no name and no label; no one hated Willie, and no one particularly liked him, either. Willie was Willie, nobody's enemy and nobody's friend. Names stick, bad names, good names and no names. It was all part of growing up, and somehow, Willie figured, when you are grown-up, there are fewer problems to deal with, fewer names to fear. Somehow, once you pass a certain age, God erases from the blackboard of your sins whatever there is written against you, and He will drill into you from some gadget in the sky, all of the things you need to know to have a happy life. God snaps His fingers or presses a button and you are no longer Willie, but William S. Heinemann, man.

* * *

Often Middlebaum visited Rip's nice blue-trimmed house on the outskirts of Squirrel Hill where they would sit in the back yard on a flagstone patio talking and playing until dinner time. While Willie watched, Middlebaum would sometimes disappear. He would disintegrate right in front of Willie's eyes, particle-by-particle, starting with his hair and ending up with his left big toe. And for a minute, Willie would think that Middlebaum had finally died and gone to heaven. Yet, Rip would continue to talk, his lips moving like nothing had happened, and Willie would have to blink and blink and slap his forehead to get Ronald Middlebaum to reappear. Willie wondered why Rip didn't notice when Middlebaum momentarily died. And he wondered how many times he would have the power to bring Middlebaum back with a knock on the forehead and a blink of the eye.

One day Middlebaum and Rip were playing football. Rip was throwing and Middlebaum was catching—or trying to catch. For though his legs were long, he simply wasn't able to coordinate the act of running and catching simultaneously. He couldn't run unless he kept his eyes on the ground, but when he watched the ground, he wasn't able to keep track of the ball.

Middlebaum centered the ball to Rip. Rip dropped back into the pocket to pass. Middlebaum ran out to catch. But sometimes

Middlebaum fell down before he could get to the ball, or the ball hit him in the back of the head before he remembered to turn around, or it went through his legs, or it bounced off his stomach when he reached out to catch it. When Middlebaum did manage to catch the ball, it was usually in an enormous suffocating hug, collecting the pigskin in his hands and arms, embracing it against his chest.

Rip, on the other hand, had great form, the way he dropped back into the pocket after the snap, then gradually rolled out. And he nearly always threw on target. Although his passes were high and soft, lacking velocity, his arm was steady, his eye precise. Willie was impressed. Rip was the only person Willie had ever seen throwing a football and wearing glasses at the same time.

It took plenty of courage for Willie to do what he did next. He had been hiding behind a clump of bushes on top of a hill, overlooking Rip's back yard. When Middlebaum centered and went out for a pass, and Rip dropped back into the pocket, his arm cocked to throw, Willie suddenly jumped up and streaked down the hill. The ball was already in the air when Willie went into action—jack-knifing right in front of Middlebaum's outstretched arms and gathering-in the ball with sure hands.

"Son of a bitch!" Middlebaum yelled in amazement, bouncing up and down.

"Holy shit!" screeched Rip. He pulled off his horn-rimmed spectacles and doffed them at Willie like a hat.

Willie got up without a word, embarrassed, but proud. He handed the ball to Rip.

"Ladies and gentlemen," Middlebaum, still bouncing, announced into his fist, "that was the most amazing catch I have ever seen in my 50 years of broadcasting professional football. Who is this new rookie?"

"Do it again," said Rip. "I'll bet you can't do it again."

Shrugging nonchalantly, but nervous inside, Willie climbed back up the hill and got himself set at the bushes. Middlebaum centered and Rip faded back, tossing a perfect spiral, with Willie rumbling down the hill and diving, this time surprising even himself by snaring the ball with one hand, landing in the grass and rolling to a game-winning touchdown on the flagstone.

Willie had never been considered much of an athlete. He didn't know why, because when he played by himself in his basement and back yard, he seemed to be pretty good. At first, he thought it was just a question of proving himself at the Herbert Hoover play-ground, but no matter how well he did one day, his accomplishments were always forgotten the next. For pick-up games, when teams were almost full and it was evident kids would be left over, everyone would jump up and down and yell, "Pick me! Pick me!" But Willie never did. There was something degrading about this. People should have already known how good he was. All they had to do was open up their eyes. Why did he have to go around tooting his own horn and begging?

Maybe it was because Willie didn't look like a good player. He was a little too short, his ass too big and dumpy. He did not move like an athlete either. When Zeewee and Kenner trotted across the play-ground, muscles danced, but when Willie ran, he waddled. It was how you look and who you know, Willie had once heard his father say. That's the way to get ahead.

They played some more. When Willie made a good catch, Rip and Middlebaum screamed and pounded him on the back. "Holy cow, ladies and gentlemen of the jury, this is the greatest football player in the world, except for Lynn Chandnois, star halfback of the Pittsburgh Steelers. Let's have a nice round of applause for this new rookie pass-catching sensation."

This attention made Willie feel really good. Even when Willie missed a catch, Middlebaum and Rip would get excited and yell, "Nice try, nice try, what a great second effort by Willie the Heinemann." It occurred to Willie that Rip had never played football before with someone who could catch because Rip didn't understand that Willie wouldn't be making those amazing catches if the ball weren't thrown accurately. Immediately, Willie decided to organize a pick-up game comprised of him at halfback and Rip at quarterback to go up to the school playground some Saturday afternoon and wipe out the Greenfield opposition. But Willie was so thrilled with all the attention he was getting, he didn't think of mentioning the plan to Rip. In fact, except for a nod or occasional grunt, Willie didn't mention anything at all. Even when Mrs. Silver served glasses of lemonade, Willie was only able to manage a shy "thank you."

Mrs. Silver had a soft, soothing voice and wore brown oxfords with white socks. "Take your time drinking," she said to Rip, "but then you'll have to come inside and get ready for dinner."

It amazed Willie to hear Rip saying, "Yes, mother," and to see him smiling even when she combed back his hair with her fingers and kissed him on the freckles. At Willie's house, there would be no lemonade, just water or, with luck, Coke. His mother would be constantly hollering about not making a mess in the kitchen, and no one would be allowed ice, because ice makes a mess and gives you a sore throat. Of course, no one could really enjoy a cold drink without sucking the ice, and you could get Pepsi or Coke anywhere. But lemonade was hand-made.

When Rip went inside, Willie and Middlebaum walked away in silence. They did not say "goodbye" or "see you later" and, although they were heading in the same direction, they followed different trails home.

It was a quiet night. Willie ate dinner, took a shower, watched TV with his parents. Nobody argued. He went to bed early and, for the first time in a long time, slept the whole night through.

Sometime during the night, the dream train came rolling by. God got off at the depot, lugging a suitcase, which He carefully set down and opened up. As Willie watched, God took out a helmet and a set of shoulder pads, put them on, produced a football and started throwing passes to Middlebaum. But Middlebaum kept dropping the ball. Each time God threw, Middlebaum dropped the ball.

As time passed, God became increasingly exasperated with Middlebaum's inept ball-handling. Finally, He told Willie to help Middlebaum out. Willie put his arm around Middlebaum's narrow shoulders and patiently explained the professional secrets of pass-catching until Middlebaum got it straight. Soon, God slapped Middlebaum on the ass, and told him to get out there, and this time to get one for the Gipper. Willie figured that the Gipper was the nickname for God.

Looking just like Otto Graham of the Cleveland Browns in his white uniform, square shoulder-pads and helmeted-head, God called the signals.

Ready!

Set!

Hike!

Willie, at center, snapped the ball to God, who dropped back into the pocket. Middlebaum ran deep for the pass, toward the goal posts. God the Gipper cocked His arm and threw. Middlebaum was in the end zone, waiting for the ball, ready to score the game-winning TD. Willie watched, but the closer the ball got to Middlebaum, the more the ball looked like a grenade. Willie tried to yell and warn Middlebaum not to touch the ball, but God paper-clipped Willie's lips. When Middlebaum finally gathered the ball in with his arms and embraced it against his stomach, the ball detonated, blowing him to pieces.

Chapter III

Friends

Willie woke up. He had been riding the dream train, and when he left the sleep, it was with a start that took him from the pillow and under the blankets to standing upright on the floor in one jerky, bounding movement. The window was open and he stuck his head through the slats of the Venetian blinds, pretending he was a prisoner in the Zenda jail, craning for a breath of life-giving fresh air. The night was warm, the stars already fading, the moon old and paling. He stood for a long time, watching the arrival of the new day and thinking about Middlebaum, feeling sad and sorry that he was going to die, sad that he was so unhappy in a life that would end before it could get better.

Willie had been toying with the idea of helping Middlebaum shape himself up with what time he had left. It wasn't clear to Willie exactly what he would tell Middlebaum, and maybe that was why he hadn't yet confronted him. Maybe subconsciously, Willie was still trying to formulate something sensible to say, and following Middlebaum around was like doing a research paper, gathering material and knowing the facts, as Miss Slippers might say, before coming to any conclusion. But it occurred to Willie that perhaps Middlebaum's life wasn't as bad as it appeared. At least Middlebaum had Rip, a friend with a nice house near Squirrel Hill, somebody to talk to. Middlebaum wasn't alone like Willie. Who am I to give advice? If my life were so good and I were so smart, I'd have better things to do than follow an almost dead person around. True, Middlebaum was going to die, but there was still someone to care about him dying. Maybe Middlebaum is better off than I am, maybe he should be doing the following around and the feeling bad for me. Something had to be done, for Middlebaum and himself.

*   *   *

Willie hurried out of school and waited for Middlebaum. It was sunny, but the early October wind huffed through Willie's cotton jacket. All day, Willie had been trying to decide what to do about Middlebaum, if anything. After all, Middlebaum was not his responsibility. Rip was Middlebaum's one and only friend, so Middlebaum was Rip's responsibility. Rip and Middlebaum's parents were the ones who had to worry, not Willie. Why should he care whether someone he hardly knew and probably didn't like was going to die? Would Middlebaum care if Willie was going to die? He didn't know, but thought that he would want someone to care, someone to talk to, who would do things for him after he was dead, like meeting Ralph Kiner, shooting Zeewee in the stomach with a .45 calibre automatic, or taking Miss Slippers out on a date.

The latter was of the utmost importance, since probably every boy in the school was deeply in love with Miss Slippers. Just today, someone had drawn the shape of a heart in chalk on Miss Slippers's chair and, when she sat down to read, the heart was transferred onto her tight black skirt that clung to her Jane Russell rear end. How wonderful to see her walk that day, the beautiful Miss Slippers, watching the heart sway, as if it were waving to every boy in the room, saying in secret semaphore, "I love you, I love you, I love only you, my Willie."

Sitting in the front of the room everyday, Willie could look underneath Slippers's desk to see her dangling ankles, her flaming red-painted toes. Sometimes she wore a clinging, powder blue Lana Turner sweater to go with her Jane Russell ass. Willie could see the shining tips of her black brassiere where the points of the breasts spread the stitches of the sweater.

Slippers was a beautiful woman and, among other things, could have made it big as the wife of a baseball player. Her voice was soft; when she talked, out flowed a gentle, rolling melody. "Osmosis," "photosynthesis," "Washington crossing the Delaware" were songs when Slippers sang them. When they rolled from her lips, Willie was hardly able to control himself, he loved her so much. Willie dreamed about getting older, so that he could legally qualify for a date with Miss Slippers. This was one of his greatest hopes.

As Willie loitered at the front of the building, Middlebaum and Rip walked out of school, talking. Willie leaned against a telephone pole to watch. After a while, they said goodbye, but Willie waited until Rip got down the street and out of earshot. Then he turned toward Middlebaum's bouncing back and took a deep breath. "Hey, Middlebaum, wait up."

"Hi," Willie said, as he walked up.

"Hi."

Willie noticed Middlebaum was wearing his heavy winter woolen pea jacket with a sweater under it. "How come you wear so many clothes?" he said.

"My mother makes me. She says I'm sickly, prone to colds." Middlebaum was watching Willie closely, seemingly bracing himself for one of Willie Heinemann's famous punches to Middlebaum's shoulder.

"Don't worry, Middlebaum. I'm not going to punch you right now."

"Then what do you want?"

"I want to know why you wear so many clothes."

"I *said* because my mother makes me. She thinks it will keep me healthy. You think I want to wear all these clothes?"

"I don't wear 15 sweaters and 12 pairs of pants, and I don't get colds."

"It's not that many. Besides, you'd wear them if your mother told you."

Willie thought for a while. "I guess if she made me," he admitted.

They started up the street, walking toward Middlebaum's house. Willie glanced around to see if anybody was watching, but no one was around. Although he was willing to consider friendship with Middlebaum, he wasn't at all willing to let anyone know about it—especially the kids from Greenfield.

"So," said Willie, as they walked. Middlebaum was very tall. Willie was at eye-level with the ping pong ball that twitched in the boy's throat.

"Yeah," Middlebaum said back.

"What's new?" Willie asked.

Middlebaum shrugged.

"Shit," said Willie.

Middlebaum nodded. "Fuck."

"Cunt," said Willie.

"Bitch," said Middlebaum.

"Bastard."

"Crapballs," Middlebaum concluded.

As they turned down Derban, Willie began to wonder what to do if Middlebaum suddenly decided to drop dead at his feet. There was only one thing, he immediately concluded. He would just keep walking along nonchalantly, pretending not to notice. There was no use getting involved.

"Didn't she look wonderful today?" Middlebaum said.

"Who?"

"Slippers."

"Yeah."

"She's beautiful." Middlebaum shook his head and rolled his raisin eyes. "Someday I'm going to marry her."

"Me too."

They were in front of Middlebaum's house now.

"You want to come up?"

"I've got to get home," Willie lied. He wouldn't have minded spending more time with Middlebaum, but didn't want to get any closer to the cooking cabbage; from where he stood, the odor tweaked his nose.

"Well then, I'll see you."

"Yeah, I'll see you around."

Willie turned and walked slowly down Derban. He was not at all afraid, had no reason to be nervous, but as soon as he turned the corner and got out of sight, he started to run, faster and faster, gaining speed downhill, pumping and puffing uphill, not stopping to rest or to allow his breath to catch up with his body until he was at home in his room, the door closed, the windows open, his blinds down, the radio blaring.

*   *   *

Then they were friends and met everyday.

Often, on the way to school, Rip would review with Middlebaum what he thought Slippers would be discussing that day, and Middlebaum would nod and ask questions about some points he didn't understand. Listening carefully, Willie was surprised at how much of the material he had forgotten, and even more surprised at how much Rip remembered. Yet, Rip wasn't really as smart as everybody thought. He was smart, all right, but not naturally. Rip could not reel off answers to everything. Often, he consulted the book. The really big difference, Willie realized, between smart kids like Rip and dumb ones like Middlebaum, was that Rip could read better, could understand what the books were telling him better than most everyone else.

Middlebaum, however, would spend hours on only a couple of pages, going back and forth to the dictionary for almost every other sentence, reading paragraphs again and again, trying to understand what each meant. Middlebaum's determination impressed Willie. If something seemed too difficult, Willie would usually go on to something else. But Middlebaum never gave up; until he mastered one sentence, he refused to move to the next; until he solved problem three, he wouldn't proceed to four. Willie never criticized this method of learning. He didn't yet feel close enough to have the authority to do so. Willie was still an outsider, and he kept his place, a singular and sometimes lonely place, responding only when he thought he should or sensed that they expected it; he was mostly more of an observer than anything else, but still he felt closer and more comfortable with these two strange boys, than with anyone else.

And with Middlebaum and Rip, Willie learned a few things.

Middlebaum was saying one day, for example, how every time he got near enough to Slippers to smell her perfume, his dick hardened up.

"He means *penis*," Rip smiled and nodded at Willie, and Willie smiled and nodded back, although he hadn't the slightest idea what Rip was talking about.

"What's *pee-niss?*" Middlebaum asked.

Almost immediately, Willie had learned that Middlebaum was stupid enough to admit when he didn't understand something. So whenever Rip mentioned something unfamiliar, Willie waited until Middlebaum asked for clarification. If Middlebaum understood, then Willie remained silent, not wanting to publicly admit that he knew less than Middlebaum.

"That's the official word for your dick," said Rip.

And because Willie could grasp something more quickly than Middlebaum, he would add to the information, and they would think that he had known all along.

"It's the same with 'schmuck' or 'cock,' *penis* is the official way to say it."

"*Pee-niss,*" Middlebaum tried it out again.

"Penis," said Willie.

"Penis," confirmed Rip.

"I don't know what *fuck* means, either, even though we say it all the time," Middlebaum admitted. "I have an idea, but I'm not so sure. I have a general picture."

"I don't know for sure, either," Rip said.

"Me too." Willie's ignorance was safe in numbers.

"My father almost explained it to me once," Rip said. "But when I started asking questions, he got too embarrassed to continue. It has something to do with the man putting his penis inside the woman."

"I think women are made like kangaroos," Middlebaum said. "My father has some magazines with pictures of naked girls in them. The girls have a hairy pocket to put their penises in."

"Fuck is a beautiful thing," said Rip. "That's all my father kept saying when I started asking questions. He kept saying, 'You'll see, it's a beautiful thing, you'll see.'"

"I'd like to fuck Slippers," said Willie.

"Boy-oh-boy, would I like to fuck her," Middlebaum giggled.

"Fuck is a beautiful thing," said Rip.

Chapter IV
Kiner's Dugout

Beechwood Boulevard followed a narrow valley between two hills. At one point, the bridge zoomed out from the middle of one hill across Beechwood to the middle of the other. Above the bridge was Murray Avenue, but under Murray and over Beechwood was a shade-soaked clearing hidden from the street and the sidewalk, fenced in by a wasteland of weeds, rocks and jagger bushes.

It was cool and dry under that bridge, the rain would never wet it. There was a different smell, a musty smell, like old newspapers in the attic. From here, they could peer way up Beechwood Boulevard, see the tops of the trees and the colors of the roofs of some of the biggest, highest houses in the classiest parts of Squirrel Hill. Turning in the other direction, they could look down into the hollow, Greenfield, where Zeewee and Kenner lived and played by the river under fiery stacks of sooty smoke.

"Wow," said Middlebaum.

"This is perfect," said Rip.

"No one knows about it except me," Willie said. "I was exploring one day. I was using the lid of a garbage can as a shield, and I was swordfighting the jagger bushes with a baseball bat, battling my way through. I wanted to touch the actual bottom of the bridge, you know? Where the foundation hits the ground? Everybody touches the top of a bridge with their feet, but hardly anybody ever thinks of touching the bottom. So, accidentally, I found this place. Look," he said, walking over to the ledge overlooking the street and pointing. "You can see almost everything happening in half of Greenfield and Squirrel Hill from here, and no one can see you. I checked it out from every angle, above and below. Nobody can see in here, and no one goes in here, either. I spent a whole week last summer hiding in the bushes, waiting for someone. But nobody came. I think we're the only people to have been here since the bridge was built. This is Pittsburgh's last secret hiding place. If we were outlaws, this would be the Badlands, where our gang could hide after robbing the Wells Fargo office."

"That's remarkable," said Rip.

"We should build a line shack," said Willie.

"What's a line shack?" Middlebaum wanted to know.

"I don't know. But on TV, the cowboys sleep in line shacks when they're working fence. And when there's a big blizzard, line shacks always save them from dying in the snow. They're very handy. I think it must be a shack built on a straight line."

"We can't build a line shack without knowing exactly what it is," said Rip. "It stands to reason. The Egyptians didn't build the pyramids without knowing what a pyramid was."

"Then let's build a pyramid."

"Let's build a castle with dragons and a moat."

The boys were silent for a while, until Willie said: "We *should* build something. We should have a place to go where there's privacy."

"Privacy is wonderful," said Middlebaum. "I love privacy."

"My parents are always bothering me," said Willie.

"My parents are always looking through my books and papers," said Rip.

"Zeewee would never find me here," said Middlebaum.

"We should build a cabin," Willie suggested.

"A little bungalow with a white picket fence."

"Wait a minute," said Rip, "we've got to be practical. If we build a cabin, then we'll have to do a lot of sawing and hammering. People would hear us and come to investigate. And also, if we had a cabin, the chimney would stick up over the bushes and weeds. People might see from the street."

"So what should we do?"

"We go underground. We dig a hole. We make a dugout. Like at the ballpark, a hole as large as a room."

"A dugout like Kiner sits in before he goes up to the plate to hit a homerun."

"A huge dugout," said Rip, "with a table and chairs, and a picture of Kiner on the wall. And we'll put a trap door on it, so nobody can ever find it. Everybody can see a cabin, but nobody can see a hole in the ground when it's covered with a trap door."

"We'll plant flowers on the trap door and people will think it's a garden," said Willie. "I got a package of zinnia seeds at home that came in the mail."

"We'll plant vegetables," said Middlebaum. "We'll have a farm."

"But then Zeewee and the Cattlemen's Association will come after us because we'd be ruining their grazing land with crops," said Willie. "There'll be a range war."

"OK, we'll just plant flowers," Middlebaum conceded. "Even the Cattlemen's Association can't be against flowers."

"Especially if they can't see them."

"I'll make the blueprints," Rip volunteered. "We'll know exactly what we're going to do from beginning to end. There won't be any mistakes or wasted time."

"We won't be able to dig the dugout until next spring because the ground is getting too hard," said Willie. It was November already.

On the way home, Rip pointed out how many things there were to do. Rip, the architect, would work on the plans, while Willie, chief carpenter, and Middlebaum, boss of the chain gang, gathered the materials they would need for building and digging in the spring. They would have to steal empty orange, cantaloupe and honeydew crates from Kalson the grocer. They would have to take each crate apart carefully, pulling out nails, to salvage as many long, flat pieces of wood as possible. Middlebaum said he only had a couple of weeks of freedom remaining until he'd be locked up in the house for winter. But Willie pointed out that if they worked hard enough after school and on weekends, they'd surely collect the materials on time. Rip agreed, said he would start on the drawings immediately, that night. Then everybody, pledging secrecy about their dugout and the hiding place under the bridge, started home.

Willie and Rip and Middlebaum walked up Beechwood Boulevard. The sun dripped through shadowy, half-bare trees making yellow patches on the gray sidewalk. Once in a while, a car would pass or a kid would ride by on his bike, and Willie would move closer to his two new friends. It was nice to be part of something after so long being part of nothing. The three boys kicked at neat little mounds of leaves that people had raked. Their shoes scattered the leaves across the sidewalk, the wind lifting them into the street.

All the while, Willie wondered whether Middlebaum would actually be around in the spring to help them dig. He counted off the months—November, December, January, February, March, April—figuring that the earliest Middlebaum would die was May. At least then, Middlebaum would have his privacy. There could be nothing more private than being buried in a box underneath a cemetery.

That night in bed, Willie saw himself digging Middlebaum's grave. The cemetery was located under the Beechwood Boulevard Bridge, and the casket in which Middlebaum rested was made from orange, cantaloupe and honeydew melon crates stolen from Mr. Kalson.

*   *   *

It was the last night on which Middlebaum was allowed to be out before his winter interment. It was very dark, and scatterings of snowflakes danced like butterflies in the light made by the lamps in the street. The two boys crept stealthily through the back yards behind Beechwood Boulevard, hugging the shadows cast by the bushes, trees and houses. Middlebaum had his pea jacket on, a leather cap with earmuffs, and four-buckle arctic boots. Willie was wearing a jacket and tennis shoes. Each carried an empty cantaloupe crate.

They knew the trail well, and it was very exciting, dashing through back yards, pretending to be an advance patrol of the U.S. Marines, recently encamped near the Halls of Montezuma, now invading Communist China, bringing truth and justice and the American way of life to the lawless yellow people. They walked through "Darlene Draper—made of paper's" back yard, climbed onto a garbage can, tiptoed across the top of a brick wall, and scrambled onto the roof of Mrs. Crowley's garage. The boxer dog, hooked to a leash long enough to protect every square inch of Crowley property, followed the two boys with shining, evil eyes. Willie selected a large rock from their storehouse of ammunition on the roof and hurled it. The boxer, drooling spittle, yelped when the rock skidded by him and retreated. Middlebaum jumped down to Crowley property, and when the dog bolted after him, Willie beaned it with another rock, chasing it back. Then Willie jumped down himself, dashing into the clear.

They cut through Willie's back yard next, then Sapienza's, then the Kelly's, over the fence and around the Glaze's house, and through the forest that was periodically saved from destruction by ranger-firefighter Ronald (The Hose) Middlebaum. Then the Abuzzi's.

The Abuzzis were Jewish, but because they were dark-complected, Willie's father insisted that they were not official Jews, but Algerian or Hindu Jews. Whatever kind of Jew she was, however, Mrs. Abuzzi was undoubtedly the most beautiful Jew in the world. Short and curvy, she wore spike-heeled shoes with ankle straps and open toes, and painted her long toenails and fingernails with different shades of frosted colors.

Willie's and Middlebaum's circuitous route finally led them to the Beechwood Boulevard Bridge. Using a flashlight, they checked out their wood supply and decided that there would be enough for their needs in the spring. In celebration, they smoked a Lucky Strike cigarette that Middlebaum had stolen last year from his mother's purse and saved for a special occasion. It tasted terrible, but Willie and Middlebaum liked the way they could make their mouths resemble smoking cannons firing volleys at pirate ships in the Red Sea.

After the cigarette, they started for home, but while passing the Abuzzi house, they heard music, the same kind of wild, rhythmic music Willie had heard played in restaurants with rugs that hang on walls. Curious, Willie and Middlebaum sneaked up the driveway, all the while aware that the music could simply be a ploy concocted by Zeewee and his men to ambush them. But they quickly forgot Zeewee and Kenner and the rest of the Greenfield gang when they peered into the window. It was fairly dark inside, but they could easily see Mrs. Abuzzi, sitting alone on the floor, in the middle of her bedroom. In the light coming from the hallway, her skin was golden and creamy. Her white slip and bra glowed fluorescently. She had nothing else on.

Willie and Middlebaum were entranced. They could not move. Even if the atomic bomb that was dropped by President Harry Truman on Hiroshima was dropped on them, they would not have been able to move. Even if the atomic bomb, along with President

Harry Truman and Hiroshima were dropped on them, they could not have moved an inch.

Mrs. Abuzzi was painting her toenails very carefully with frosted polish. The restaurant-with-rugs-on-the-wall-music played on the phonograph, and every time she finished a toenail, Mrs. Abuzzi raised a golden delicious leg and stroked it lavishly from ankle to thigh. Then, with the song almost over, she stood up and walked over to the victrola to play the record again, all the while weaving her ivory ass like a hula dancer. She slowly returned to her spot on the floor, squeezed her ass with frosty-tipped fingers as she sank down and rubbed against the rug, before selecting another toe to frost.

Willie and Middlebaum watched for a very long time. It seemed like only a second and, at the same time, seemed like forever to the two boys, as they watched, hungering for those fantastic toes, until she finished both feet, shut off the light, and undulated from the room. They sat for a while, their hearts beating crazily, their hands clutching their penises, which were pulsating wildly, inexplicably all perked up like pickles. Then, they started for home.

Willie and Middlebaum said goodbye for the winter. They would see each other in school, of course, but it wouldn't be the same. Middlebaum said he usually got sick in the winter. Willie said you could never tell, but that he might get sick, too. Middlebaum said they could talk to each other on the telephone.

Willie wondered what number to call if the person you are calling is dead.

Chapter V
Winter Games, Funny Names

Winter was the jailer, the worst time of the year for Willie because it left him no alternative but to be inside, inside home, school, himself. Winter meant four-buckle arctic boots, heavy coats and itchy woolen sweaters. Winter was repetition. You waited until the last possible moment, then closed your eyes, gritted your teeth, left your house, and leaned into the wind toward school. You went right to your homeroom, and some days you'd only see Rip and Middlebaum in the bathroom or in class, sitting on the other side of the map of the United States of America. You did that every day, day after day.

Winter was the time to plan for the days when the winter went away. Middlebaum found a recipe for beer in one of his father's copies of *Fling* Magazine. "We'll make beer," Middlebaum decided, "a whole ton of it."

"And we'll invite girls down to the dugout," said Willie.

"Not until it's built," Rip cautioned with a wagging forefinger. "Not until the whole thing is finished and looks like a fancy saloon. Then we'll bring the girls."

"We'll call it the Kiner Cafe," said Willie. "We'll invite some sexy girls, put on the radio and dance."

"Boy-oh-boy," said Middlebaum.

"Then we'll get drunk," said Rip. "We'll make the girls drunk, tell them to close their eyes and open their mouths for a kiss, and we'll pour quarts of beer down their throats before they realize what's happening."

"They'll be plastered!"

"And then," said Rip, "we'll fuck 'em."

"We'll fuck 'em to pieces," said Middlebaum.

"We'll fuck 'em like they never been fucked before," confirmed Rip.

Winter was also a time for changing.

Once, when Slippers was sick, a substitute teacher took over for the day and decided to rearrange the seating chart in alphabetical order.

"What's your name?"

"Hiddlebaum," said Middlebaum.

"Then you move over beside Heinemann."

"What'd you do that for?" Willie whispered when Hiddlebaum sat down.

"So I could sit next to you."

"What's your name?" the teacher asked Willie.

"Irwin Scabb."

"Well, you don't belong next to Hiddlebaum, you're next to Schwartz."

"Schwartz? Who's Schwartz?"

"That's me!" yelled Rip.

Winter was invention.

Sometimes, on Saturday afternoons, Willie and Rip went to Middlebaum's house. There, they could pretend that Kiner was their father. They called Ralph "Dad."

Winter was the worst after bedtime, for Willie could never get to sleep. It was too dark and scary to sleep. People and things could sneak up on him when he was least expecting it if he were sleeping, and he would never see them coming or sense their presence until it was much too late. He was always being ambushed by his ulcer in the darkness. So he could not sleep; he could only wait in the dark and hope to sleep before the ulcer got him.

Night after night, Willie waited for the ulcer to strike, watching the shadows of the ghosts and goblins, or the boogeyman and boogeywoman dance on the ceiling or rest on the Venetian blind. Willie waited, and while he waited, he pretended he was in a mine shaft, buried alive after being poisoned by Communist Chinese spies who had infiltrated the neighborhood, disguised as Algerian Jews. Willie set his wastebasket on top of his dresser, tied his socks into knots and shot baskets. He sneaked down to the basement in his pajamas and golfed rolls of toilet paper through the coal bin door with a broomstick. He wedged his pillow upright against the wall, in the corner on his bed, and boxed it for the heavyweight championship of the world. He sang Stephen Foster songs to the slaves in the South who were digging their way to Pennsylvania on the underground railroad. Time passed. The truth of the matter was that Willie could not sleep without first playing a game, or a couple of games, to make himself tired and to get his mind off his ulcer and the other enemies he feared. He spent a lot of time inventing new games to practice during the day, so that he could use them during the night, to make him weary enough to sleep, before the ulcer got him.

This winter, there was also something missing that had not been missing before: his friends. Willie was not unaware of the irony of the situation. He had befriended Middlebaum because Middlebaum was lonely and sad and on the threshhold of death. He had befriended Middlebaum because of his conviction that Middlebaum would need comfort and company. But now, suddenly, he seemed to need Middlebaum as much as Middlebaum needed him. There is nothing wrong with being lonely as long as you have never been anything else. But once you've discovered companionship, then the loneliness is intolerable. He wished there was something he could do.

* * *

Three things happened that made the winter better, however. The first was initiated by Ronald Middlebaum.

"Here," Middlebaum said one day in school, handing Willie a small package wrapped in aluminum foil.

"What is it?"

"It's a walkie-talkie."

"Are you kidding?" Willie peeked under the foil. "There's a package of Lucky Strike cigarettes under here. You better watch it, Middlebaum," Willie warned, handing the package back, "you better not be caught with cigarettes in school."

"That's what it's disguised to look like," said Middlebaum, "cigarettes. But I'm telling you, it's really a walkie-talkie." He shoved it back into Willie's hand. "There's a built-in aerial in there. And the wires are all invisible. I painted them with invisible ink."

"This is no walkie-talkie."

"It is too. I built it. I ought to know."

"It is not."

"I'll show you," said Middlebaum. "If you don't believe me, we'll try it out right here." With his thumb, Middlebaum flicked an imaginary switch on the side of the package and made a clicking noise with his mouth. "First, you activate it with this switch," he explained. "The switch is invisible so nobody will know how to activate or deactivate except for me, you, and Kiner."

"What do you mean, Kiner?" asked Willie. "This is ridiculous. You can't talk to Kiner on this thing. You can't talk to anybody. You couldn't even talk to Kiner if it was a real walkie-talkie."

"That's what you think," said Middlebaum. "Everybody thinks I've been sick all this time, but that's not why I've been absent from school so often. It's all a big joke, a trick. I haven't been sick a day in my life. The truth is, I've been working in secret in my laboratory on this make-believe walkie-talkie."

"You see," said Willie, "even you admit it's make-believe."

"Just because it's make-believe doesn't mean it doesn't work," Middlebaum retorted.

"This is stupid," said Willie.

"Middlebaum to Willie, Middlebaum to Willie," Middlebaum barked into the cigarette package with the aluminum foil around it.

"This really is stupid," Willie said again.

"Can you hear me?" said Middlebaum.

"Yes, I can hear you. Of course, I can hear you."

"So, then it works."

"But I could hear you without the walkie-talkie."

"How do you know you can?"

"Because I hear you all the time."

"You can't hear Kiner."

"I can't hear Kiner *with* the walkie-talkie, either."

"That's what Kiner said you'd say."

"What are you talking about?"

"Kiner said that as long as you think the walkie-talkies work, they will work. But once you doubt walkie-talkie magic, its power dies. Kiner wants you to keep the make-believe walkie-talkie, Willie. He likes you a lot and wants you to call him up sometimes."

Willie went home with the make-believe walkie-talkie in his back pocket. He was depressed. He couldn't understand what had happened to Middlebaum, and wondered whether Middlebaum's disease had afflicted his brain. He had never seen his friend that insistent before.

It was an inky, icy night, early in January.

Willie watched television. He threw spitballs at his father's Bar Mitzvah picture on the mantle. He looked out the window, but except for the snow, and a steaming pile of dung dropped by Crowley's boxer dog, there was nothing to see. He called up people on the telephone and breathed into the mouthpiece. He called up Rossi's Pizza Palace and ordered a pizza with anchovies to be delivered to Kalson the grocer. He called up Kalson and ordered a jar of pickled herring, four quarts of beet borscht and three dozen bagels to be delivered to Rossi's Pizza Palace. In the living room, he tore out the last page of the book his father had been reading. He turned on the television. He turned off the television. He had dinner. He said goodnight. He went to bed.

In his room the lights were off and it was dark; the shadows sneaked past the window. He got into bed and closed his eyes. He couldn't take it any longer, this boredom and loneliness. Why didn't anybody like him? Why didn't anybody talk to him? Why didn't he ever try talking to anybody else? Then he opened his eyes, got out of bed and stared at the blank, black walls, listening to the shadows make their magic. After a while, Willie walked over to where his bluejeans hung on the bedpost and pulled from the pocket the package of cigarettes wrapped in aluminum foil Middlebaum had given him. He took it in his hand and went over to the window, then pulled up the Venetian blind and, in the light from the street lamps, searched the foil for the invisible switch. When he located it, he flicked down his thumb and clicked on his tongue. Nothing happened. He searched the package more carefully and found another switch, and flicked that down with his thumb. Again, nothing. *Damn Middlebaum, fucker Middlebaum, shithead Middlebaum,* Willie thought. Suddenly, just as he was about to give up, Willie could hear the invisible wires buzzing in secret frequency. He couldn't believe it, but it was happening all the same, just as Middlebaum had promised. Then he said, "Willie calling Kiner, Willie calling Kiner, Willie calling Kiner."

There was nothing, except the buzzing of the secret frequency, but now he felt the walkie-talkie warming in his hands.

"This is Willie Heinemann calling Ralph Kiner. This is Willie Heinemann calling Ralph Kiner. This is Willie Heinemann calling

Ralph Kiner. Are you there, Mr. Kiner? Over."

Nothing yet, but now the walkie-talkie was cooking and humming in Willie's palm.

"Willie to Kiner, Willie to Kiner, Willie to Kiner. Are you there, Mr. Kiner? Please, Mr. Kiner, are you there? Over."

Still there was nothing, and Willie waited, staring at the walkie-talkie in his hand, listening to the beat of hope in his heart. Then came a crackling, like somebody rolling up paper, and some wheezing and coughing, and more crackling from rolling up paper, and after the crackling, came Kiner.

The voice was deep and strong, thundering through Willie like Kiner's line drives crashing against the Forbes Field center field wall. "Kiner to Willie, Kiner to Willie, Kiner to Willie. Are you there, Willie Heinemann? Are you there?"

"This is me, Mr. Kiner," said Willie. "Is this really you? Over."

"This is Ralph," said Kiner. "How you doing, Willie? Over."

"How many homeruns you going to hit this year? Over."

"I think I'll hit eighty or so. Over."

"Oh, you'll probably smash about a hundred. Over."

"I'm down here in Florida for spring training," said Kiner. "I been wanting to tell you that the Pirates got an eye on you, Willie. We've been scouting your back yard for the past couple of years. We wish you could come down and work out with us. We need better hitting, and we think you're the man for the job. Over."

"Gee, I could come down tomorrow. Over."

"You're not old enough. Wait until you get out of high school. Then you can become a Pirate. We don't want any ballplayers without any formal education. Over."

"I understand," said Willie. "Over."

"I'll be in touch," said Kiner. "Over and out."

Willie woke up the following morning with the walkie-talkie in his hand.

"I talked to Kiner last night," said Willie to Middlebaum in school.

"I know," said Middlebaum. "I talked to him, too. Kiner won't be home tonight because he's got a date with a movie star, so why don't you call me?"

"OK, I'll call you late, from in my bed."

Now Willie and Middlebaum had faith in the magic of the make-believe walkie-talkies. And for the rest of the winter, and the rest of

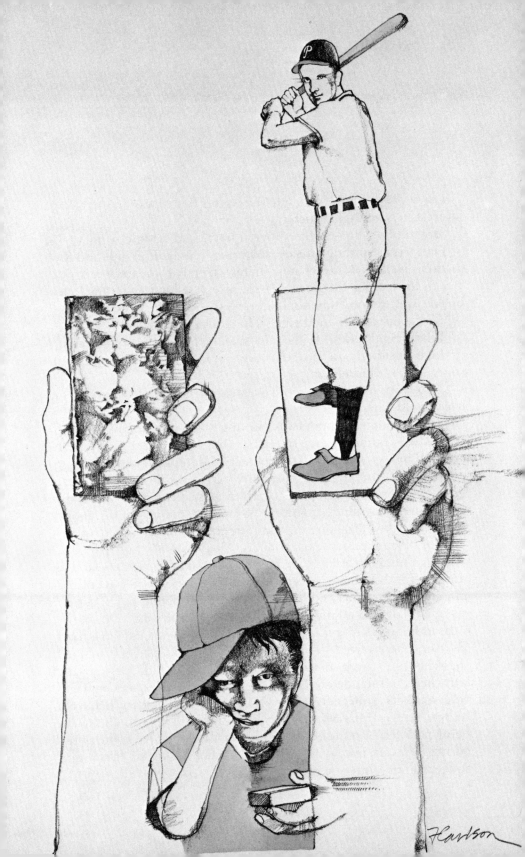

their time together, the walkie-talkies worked.

The second thing that made the winter better was an increased interest in bazoongie watching.

"Boy-oh-boy, boy-oh-boy, boy-oh-boy," said Middlebaum.

They were standing outside, shivering in the cold, Willie and Rip in their jackets, Middlebaum in his layers of sweaters, his pea jacket, his leather fur-lined gloves, his extra-long scarf, his four-buckle arctic boots, watching Slippers through the window.

"Kowabonga," moaned Rip. "That's all I can say."

"Like megaphones," Willie said, shaking his head in amazement.

"Like upside down Howard Johnson double-decker ice cream cones," said Middlebaum.

"Those are undoubtedly the greatest bazoongies that have ever lived," said Rip.

The bazoongies Slippers was showing that day were covered with red taffeta and had points so perfect they looked as if they'd been inserted in a special pencil sharpener. Middlebaum let out a long, deep sigh as the ping pong ball quivered in his throat. "I'm sorry you guys ever introduced me to bazoongies," he said. "I can hardly get them off my mind anymore. Bazoongies are all I think about, night and day, bazoongies. Last night at dinner, I said to my mother, 'Please pass the bazoongies.' She was really angry."

Each Thursday at Herbert Hoover, the sixth grade reported to the gym for dancing lessons given by Miss Sparks, who was tall and muscular, with arms and legs resembling telephone poles, closely cropped hair and a long, narrow, carrot-colored nose.

In addition to supervising dance, Sparks was the sheriff of Herbert Hoover. She scoured the playground for hooky-players, roamed the school in search of kids without hall passes, and periodically launched commando raids into the boys' bathroom seeking cigarette smokers, gum chewers, candy eaters. When a kid misbehaved, he was sent to Miss Sparks for punishment. This usually meant being paddled or standing in the corner watching Sparks out of the corner of your eye as she ate her bushel basket of lunch and squeezed her white sponge ball.

Whenever Willie, Rip, Middlebaum or anyone else would see her, Sparks would always be squeezing this white sponge ball. And all the while she was squeezing, she would smile and wink, wrinkle up her carrot-colored nose, smile and wink, on and on. She would do this, no matter where she might be, until a kid just couldn't help but to smile and wink right back at her. Then, Sparks would immediately retract her smile and walk away, leaving the kid standing all alone, grinning and winking and wrinkling his nose like a fool.

For the regular Thursday dance class, when boys and girls danced together, alone, Sparks always brought out her two favorite records, Kay Starr's "Wheel of Fortune," and "Three Coins in the Fountain," by Old Blue Eyes Sinatra. Sparks played these records over and over, waltzing around the room all by herself, winking and smiling, wrinkling her nose and squeezing her white sponge ball, as she demonstrated the high points of the box step. When this happened, Rip paired himself with Shirley Millmaker, and Middlebaum, the tallest, skinniest boy in the class, got with Laurel Gibson, who was only two inches taller and five pounds skinnier. Willie, meanwhile, cuddled up with Bernadine Levine. He didn't know what to say to a girl—especially a girl with a mouth full of braces that glowed in the dark—but he liked Bernadine and thought she liked him. Once, Bernadine actually told Willie that she loved him. Willie said he loved her, too. But the very next time they saw each other, he ran away. On February 12, he mailed Bernadine Levine a Valentine's Day card, but didn't sign his name. He also mailed Slippers and Abuzzi Valentine's Day cards, but he signed Miss Sparks's name.

After the music started and everyone paired up, Sparks would continue to glide across the room, holding an imaginary partner in her arms, doing the box step, squeezing her sponge ball, keeping time for the boys.

"One, two, three, four . . . one, two, three, four . . . one, two, three, four . . . not a triangle, not a rectangle, not a circle. Do a box, a perfect box."

Sparks smiled and sang and winked and wrinkled her nose. Sometimes, she'd close her eyes, and Willie could see her lips moving to the words of the song, especially when it was "Three Coins in the Fountain." Around and around, Willie and Rip and Middlebaum and the rest of the boys and girls whirled, with Sparks's lips moving in unison with the crooning lyrics from Old Blue Eyes.

Willie hadn't noticed before, but seeing them together, he discovered that Laurel Gibson bounced when she walked, or at least when she danced, just like Middlebaum. And when they weren't tripping over one another, Laurel and Middlebaum trampolined along together in perfect harmony.

"They look cute, don't they?" Bernadine Levine whispered to Willie through her stainless steel teeth.

"Who?"

"Middlebaum and Laurel."

"Middlebaum cute?"

"Laurel thinks Middlebaum is a doll," Bernadine told Willie.

"Laurel Gibson thinks you're a doll," Willie told Middlebaum later that day.

"Me? A doll? She thinks I'm a doll?"

"That's what Bernadine says."

"Gee." The ping pong ball danced up and down in unison with Middlebaum's bouncing body. "I think she's a doll, too, and she's got big bazoongies."

"Laurel? If you ask me, she looks flat as a board."

"That's the way she looks, but that's not the way she really is. Her bazoongies are actually the size of beach balls, but she sucks them in sometimes, like suction cups."

"I don't know about that," said Willie.

"She lets them out when we dance," said Middlebaum. "They hit me right in the neck. They're so big, they almost choke me to death."

If Middlebaum really was going to die, Willie thought, then that was the perfect way to do it.

The third thing that happened to make the winter better was the arrival of the new kid from Florida whose name was Wier Strange. There's nothing more to report about this kid, except that he got Willie, Rip and Middlebaum thinking seriously about names.

"Why don't baseball players have dumb names?" said Middlebaum. *Kiner's* not dumb. *Pee Wee Reese, Gil Hodges, Gair Allie, Howie Pollett, Ted Kluszewski,* those are good names. I'd trade my

Middlebaum name for any one of those names in a minute."

"But they're baseball players," said Willie. "Only people have stupid names. You can't be a baseball player unless you have a name like Mickey Mantle, Whitey Ford, Vic Wertz."

"Yeah, and what about Duke Snider?"

"There's no better name in the world than good old Duke Snider."

"How about Richie Ashburn or Preacher Roe?"

"Or Branch Rickey?"

"I'd give my pitching arm to have a name like Branch."

"Which goes to show that the whole National League would be ruined if regular people with regular names played baseball."

"You mean like my uncle, Herman Gluck," said Middlebaum.

"Herman Gluck is a perfect example."

"ATTENTION LADIES AND GENTLEMEN," announced Middlebaum, holding his fist up to his mouth. "LEADING OFF, WITH A BATTING AVERAGE OF TWO-SEVEN-FIVE, THE SECOND BASEMAN, HERMAN GLUCK."

"AND AT SHORTSTOP," Willie announced into his own fist. "BATTING THREE-OH-ONE, ARNOLD ZLOTNICK."

"IN LEFT FIELD," barked Rip, "WITH AN AVERAGE OF ONE FIFTY-SEVEN, BATTING THIRD, LENNY MATES."

"IN THIS CORNER," Middlebaum switched the sport, "FROM SLIPPERY ROCK, PENNSYLVANIA, WEIGHING TWO HUN-DRED AND FIFTY THOUSAND POUNDS, EIGHT OUNCES, CLIFFORD KLUTZ."

"AND IN THE OPPOSITE CORNER," said Willie, "FROM LONDON, ENGLAND, WEIGHING SEVENTY-TWO THOU-SAND POUNDS EVEN, MAX TABACHNIK."

It was after school, and the weather was good for January, so they walked slowly, laughing down the street.

"Who's Max Tabachnik?" said Middlebaum.

"He's my cousin. He's married to Ethel Tabachnik."

"She plays shortstop for the Detroit Tigers," said Rip.

"No, she's the left guard for the Pittsburgh Steelers," Willie giggled. "She weighs about 350 pounds with her clothes off."

"What's she weigh with her clothes on?" asked Middlebaum.

"She can't get clothes to fit her," said Willie.

"I'll bet Herman Gluck who sells dresses at Lane Bryant can fit her up."

"Lenny Mates is a wine taster for Mogen David," said Rip. "My father knows him personally."

"What's Lenny Mates do after he tastes it?" asked Middlebaum.

"I don't know," said Rip. "My father could ask him. Sounds like a good job."

"Maybe he takes a swallow from every little bottle and waits five minutes, and if it doesn't make him throw up, they sell it to customers. I think President Eisenhower has an official eater who takes a bite out of all his food. If the official eater dies, then the President orders a different dish."

"Arnold Zlotnick doesn't exist. I made him up," Willie confessed.

"Same thing with me and Clifford Klutz," said Middlebaum.

"I'll bet he exists anyway," said Willie. "I'll bet you could make up any name and find a person somewhere in the world who actually owns it."

"How about Fuck-A-Duck?" said Middlebaum.

"That's probably a Chinese name," said Rip.

"Goose-A-Moose?"

"That could be an Indian Chief."

"Fart-A-Heart?"

"Alaskan."

"Rape-An-Ape."

"President of the Belgian Congo."

They pulled up in front of Middlebaum's house and dropped him off. Rip and Willie usually had little to talk about when Middlebaum wasn't around, but today, they discussed names. They talked all the way from Derban to Beechwood, making up names like Harry Harness, Useless S. Grunt and Hy. O. Silver.

"I wrote your uncle, Herman Gluck, a letter," Rip said to Middlebaum the following morning in school.

"You wrote Herman Gluck?"

"That's right."

"But you don't know him," said Willie.

"I looked him up in the phone book. I told him I loved him and signed the letter Ethel Tabachnik."

"I think I'll write Lenny Mates and challenge him to a duel," said Willie. "I'll tell him to meet me behind Kalson's Grocery Store and I'll sign the letter Arnold Zlotnick."

"I'm going to call up Max Tabachnik and tell him about the romance going on between his wife and Herman Gluck," said Middlebaum.

"I think the winner of the duel between Mates and Zlotnick should fight Herman Gluck," said Willie.

Pretty soon, they could talk about nothing else but Arnold Zlotnick, Lenny Mates, Ethel and Max Tabachnik and Herman Gluck. Willie and Rip even made a trip downtown one Saturday afternoon to Lane Bryant to see what Herman Gluck looked like. He was a short, bald man with a white mustache and flat feet.

In Lane Bryant, Willie walked right up to Herman Gluck and asked him the price of a certain dress. Herman Gluck said sixteen dollars. Then Willie asked if the dress would fit his mother. "My mother weighs 350 pounds and her name is Ethel," Willie told him. Herman Gluck said that this was a size 20 dress. Nobody who weighs 350 pounds could fit into a size 20 dress. Willie said that that was too bad because he only wanted to buy his mother a dress that was a size 20. Then he asked if he could try the dress on.

"On your mother?"

"No," said Willie, "on me."

Herman Gluck told Willie to get his ass out of the store.

They went to Middlebaum's house to report their adventure, but first called up Rossi's Pizza Palace and ordered a large pizza to be delivered to Herman Gluck at Lane Bryant with the name "Ethel" spelled out in pepperoni.

When they arrived, Middlebaum was sipping hot chocolate, and even though he was in his pajamas and was recuperating from his millionth cold of the winter, he was smiling.

"Guess what we just did," said Willie.

"Nnamenieh," said Middlebaum. "And Revlis."

"What are you talking about, Middlebaum?"

"Eeweez, Izzuba and Sreppils."

"Look Middlebaum, we've got something important to tell you," said Rip.

"You mean," said Middlebaum, "Muabelddim. Muabelddim is Middlebaum spelled backwards. I figured it out this afternoon. You are Nnamenieh, Willie, and Rip is Revlis. And then there's Zeewee, Abuzzi and Slippers, better known as Eeweez, Izzuba and Sreppils."

Middlebaum's discovery brought forth a whole new week of activities. They forgot about Lenny Mates, Herman Gluck, Arnold Zlotnick and the Tabachniks, except to change their names to Kculg, Setam, Kinhcabat and Kcintolz. Miss Glom, the kindergarten teacher, was Molg. Sparks was Skraps, while the art teacher was now officially known from coast-to-coast as Mr. Blot. There was Noslak's Yrecorg Store and Namrebeil's Yrekab Shop. Mrs. Yelworc's dog was a rexob. Of all the girls in school, Arabrab Knarf was their favorite.

When history was the subject in Sreppils's class, Willie and Rip and Middlebaum were busy with the Presidents of the United States, beginning with Egroeg Notgnihsaw to Maharba Nlocnil, who freed the sevals, up to Vice President Noxin, and President Rewohnesie, more commonly known as Eki. Of all the presidents, they liked Klop, Revooh, Tfat and the team of "Eonaceppit and Relyt, oot," the best.

It was now February, which seemed like the longest month of the year, even though it owned the shortest days, and the name game, for a couple of weeks, helped the winter wear away.

Chapter VI
Chauncey Is Discovered

No one knew how, when, or even why Chauncey had arrived in the neighborhood. He just appeared one day, an old black man with a dirty tweed sport coat and a once-white shirt with a half-ripped collar, flapping like a butterfly's wing at his neck. He would often disappear and then reappear, weeks or even months later, wearing the same old scuffed oxfords, dirty pants, dirtier wool watch cap, tree bark skin. No one could keep track of how many times Chauncey came and went, and no one knew where he'd go. No one could even be sure he would come back, and no one cared. But of one thing everyone could be completely certain: whenever Willie, or Rip, or Middlebaum, or anybody in the whole world saw him, Chauncey would be staggering and grunting, stumbling and mumbling, because old Chauncey was always drunk as a skunk.

Willie, and Rip, and Middlebaum had never given much thought to Chauncey (he was not important; he did not play baseball; there were no empty soda-pop bottles on his back porch to steal) until the day they discovered the one awful fact: Chauncey was the only other person in the world to know there was a place to hide, where no one could see you or find you, under the Beechwood Boulevard Bridge.

* * *

On the fateful day of Chauncey's discovery, Willie lay on his back in his bedroom, waiting for Middlebaum to arrive.

"Willie to Middlebaum, Willie to Middlebaum, Willie to

Middlebaum. Over. Are you there, Middlebaum? Over."

"This is Middlebaum. Over."

"I'm surrounded by a hostile war party of Chief Eeweez's braves. Over."

"How many are there? Over."

"I can't see them all, but they're wearing warpaint. Over."

"Roger and A-OK. I'll rescue. This is Buffalo Middlebaum, over and out."

Willie tucked the walkie-talkie into his boot, which looked like a tennis shoe, and peeked through the knothole of his fortress bedroom. One of the Indians took a potshot, but Willie ducked, crawled across the floor, and climbed into his bunk.

He heard the flaming arrows shot by Chief Eeweez's men pocking into the roof, but he wasn't worried, because the original settlers, aware of the dangers of living in the wilderness between Greenfield and Squirrel Hill, had built the house with asbestos. And asbestos, according to Slippers, was guaranteed not to burn. Waiting to be rescued by Buffalo Middlebaum, Willie thought back over the past few weeks.

As soon as the warm spring had wiped away the winter wind, Willie, Rip, and Middlebaum had started excavating Kiner's dugout under the Beechwood Boulevard Bridge. The dirt, soaking for years in the shade of those jetting concrete spires, felt good in their hands, silken, smooth and moist, easy to dig, easy as seashore sand, but better, since sand is dry and granular like sugar and won't stick together. "You couldn't dig a dugout like this on the beach because the walls could cave in," Rip explained. "But here we can make the walls and floor smooth and level."

That would come soon. Now they were just digging, filling cardboard boxes with dirt and dumping the dirt behind the bridge, concealing all evidence of construction. Willie did most of the digging because it was his shovel, and because he liked working with his hands. He didn't have to make any important decisions, all he had to do was dig, pretending he was a gravedigger, or a great and ancient builder of empires, like Leonardo daVinci, commissioned by Alexander the Great to carve a monument to the power and glory of Greenfield.

Meanwhile, Middlebaum started collecting empty soda pop bottles to trade at Kalson's for 2¢ and 5¢. Although he found many empty bottles in the streets and gutters and stole many others from neighbors, his best source of bottles came from his own kitchen. Every time his father would bring home a case of Canada Dry quarts, Middlebaum would pop open some of the tops, dump the contents down the toilet and cash in the empties.

All in all, they had a good rhythm going, with Willie digging dirt, Middlebaum collecting and stealing bottles, and Rip banking and hiding the money, making plans, and most important, guarding the secret recipe.

WITH JUST A LITTLE KNOWLEDGE, ANYONE CAN MAKE PERFECT BEER THE FIRST TIME. IT WILL BE ECONOMICAL AND TASTY. THERE'S REALLY NOTHING TO IT.

Mix eight pounds of sugar in eleven gallons of water. Stir until all of the sugar is dissolved. Add one five-pound can of Pabst Blue Ribbon Extract of Malt. Mix until the liquid turns a dark amber. Crumble-in one and a half cakes of Fleischmann's Yeast. Add one thinly-sliced potato—unpeeled. Cover the tub tightly and allow to ferment twenty-five to forty-five days. When a gray foam forms on top of the liquid, strain out any lumps of yeast and add slices of potato that remain. Many of the potato slices will dissolve into the beer. Then bottle. Brown unclear bottles are best. To aid carbonation, let stand three-to-five days before drinking. Beer is best when served chilled.

One Saturday, Rip arrived late at the construction site, cradling two big brown bags in his arms. Willie and Middlebaum gathered around and watched, while Rip, eyes sparkling, displayed his purchases.

"YEAST!"

"Yippee, all right," Middlebaum and Willie cheered.

"MALT!"

"Goddam, fuck and shit-erino."

"SUGAR!"

They lacked a pot large enough to hold the prescribed amounts, but Willie found an old washtub that would do the job. Rip dragged the tub back into the tall weeds, added the yeast and malt. Willie and Middlebaum tasted everything as Rip worked. Rip had put on his glasses to read the directions, and Willie really thought for a second that Rip was either Albert Einstein or Albert Frankenstein. He wasn't sure which. But he didn't care. It was one of the most exciting scenes he had ever witnessed. They were actually making beer. Willie would drink it and get drunk, just like the baseball players after winning the World Series or hitting a grandslam homerun. As the late afternoon sun grilled in the sky, the boys burst out laughing, not uproariously, but in tremors, poking each other's ribs, doing little dances around the tub, shoving hands in pockets, fingering penises, then urinating their excitement away into the weeds.

Willie attributed the good progress of the dugout to Rip who carried a notebook around wherever he went and wrote down everything that had to be done. Willie marveled at people like Rip and Slippers and all they knew; he couldn't imagine ever being able to remember that much. In fact, as he got older he seemed to be losing his memory. He pictured himself at 25, wandering the streets, not even remembering his own name, where he lived, or how to get there. He worried that his poor memory was perhaps a signal that he was aging too quickly, getting old and creaky like Grandmother Ida.

When Willie wasn't worrying about his lost memory or his lost youth, he was worrying about Ronald Middlebaum. No matter how hard he tried, he could hardly think of anything other than Middlebaum. Middlebaum in school or under the Beechwood Boulevard Bridge, the shadowy image of Middlebaum dying, or of Middlebaum dead, folded neatly like a towel into a footlocker and dropped into the Monongahela River. He would think about Middlebaum and that's who he would see on the screen of night in the darkest corner of his room.

Willie heard shots coming from Middlebaum's repeater rifle. He got down from his bunk, walked through the house and opened his front door. "That was a close call," he said.

"What are you talking about?" asked Middlebaum.

"Eeweez's braves were closing in. It was lucky for me I could contact you on the walkie-talkie. You saved my life."

"What?"

"You know, on the good old walkie-talkie?"

"Oh yeah, your message came in faint. I got most of it, although I can't remember anything right now."

"I told you. They were shooting fire arrows into my roof."

"So what did you do?"

"I didn't do anything. My house is made out of asbestos, you know that."

"Oh yeah, mine is, too. I forgot."

"We're lucky," said Willie.

"I know, if we lived in a thatched hut, we'd be dead a hundred times a day."

Wild Willie Hickock and Buffalo Middlebaum dropped out the back window and crawled on their bellies away from the house. Then, just in case of snipers, they made a run for it, following the trail that led to Rip's homestead on the far edge of the prairie.

The three boys hurried toward the bridge, anxious to continue their work. They went down the street, up the steps, slithered through the weeds and jagger bushes and burst into the clearing. But there he was, sprawled in the dugout with his his ass inside and his arms hanging out, Chauncey, flashing his piano key teeth, pursing his liver lips into a bow from which came an eerie, high-pitched chant: "Wooooeeeee, woooooooeeeeeeeeeeeeeee." He wailed and wailed, stopping periodically to listen to the sound boomeranging back at him from high up in the concrete rafters of the bridge. "Woooooooeeeeeeeeee oooooooeeeeee."

For a while, he didn't see Willie, Rip, or Middlebaum. And had they not been so confident of their isolation, the boys would have probably been able to scramble back under cover before being seen. But they were too surprised, stuck in their tracks, mesmerized by the sight and sound of this old black man.

Chauncey wailed, "Woooeeeeeeeooooooooeeeee," then paused and wailed and stopped and wailed and wailed again, listening to the echo of that terrible high-pitched chant, following the sound high above him as best he could with darting, black-button eyes. Suddenly, the black man looked up, saw them, and sprang at them with such quick ferocity that the boys would have surely been captured had Chauncey not immediately lost his balance and toppled back into the hole.

Chauncey tried to jump out of the dugout and again go after the boys, but his foot got caught on the edge, and he tumbled back down a second time. Finally, pulling himself up, like he was climbing out of a swimming pool, he got to his knees and to his feet, began to stagger—and then he charged. With his arms stuck out like a walking dead man, Chauncey came at them, falling to his knees, then climbing back up on his feet, all the while continuing his soulful song, which had no words and seemed to be coming from high-fidelity speakers hidden somewhere inside the bridge.

The boys were dumbfounded, unable to respond. Not until Chauncey was almost close enough to touch them, not until Willie could see the pink-white tips of Chauncey's fingers, did Willie break and run with Middlebaum and Rip close behind. They scrambled so fast and recklessly through the weeds, down the steps and up the street, that by the time they reached Rip's house, Chauncey's chants were still echoing like a warped record in the phonographs of their ears.

A few days later, they mustered up enough courage to return to the bridge. They walked down Beechwood Boulevard with their hearts trembling and Middlebaum's ping pong ball wild in his throat. When they reached the patch of bushes and weeds that concealed their hideout, they dropped down on their hands and knees and crept slowly forward, continually stopping to listen and look, before creeping a few feet closer. It took a long time before they edged their way out into the clearing.

Chauncey was there again, sitting in the half-done dugout, head back, eyes closed, but this time not wailing or grunting; seemingly, he was asleep. They watched for a while, but when Chauncey did not move or talk, Willie tossed a rock, which clattered against the concrete, to catch his attention. Willie and Rip and Middlebaum lay very still in the weeds as the coal man's eyes opened, and though he looked around carefully, he obviously did not see them because he did not move. Eventually, his eyelids dropped back down to sleeping position.

The boys retraced their steps back through the bushes and underbrush and up the street, talking in whispered short sentences until they reached Rip's patio. They sat down heavily on the squeaky blue glider. They rocked and rocked.

"That bastard, he's going to ruin all our plans," Middlebaum finally said. "We're not going to do anything we wanted to do this summer."

"I don't know of any other hiding place." Willie shook his head, a pained expression on his round face. "All the other secret places I know about, other people know about, too."

"Colored people are always looking for secret places," Middlebaum said. "They need to hide while they paint themselves white."

"They don't paint themselves, they take a knife and scrape the black off their skin," Willie theorized. "That's why a colored person's palms are always lighter than any other part of their body; it rubs away as they work."

"I wonder why their teeth aren't black."

"They must bleach them in peroxide, like Slippers does her hair."

All the while, Rip was sitting quietly and swinging back and forth on the glider, listening to his friends. "There's no other place for Kiner's dugout," he said talking slowly, lifting his bushy eyebrows. "Right?"

"Right," said Middlebaum and Willie.

"And if we don't have privacy and secrecy under that bridge, we won't have anything else to do, and it will be another rotten summer. Right?"

"Right."

"There's nothing else we can do; we have no choice," said Rip.

"Right," said Middlebaum and Willie. "We have no choice."

"We have to get rid of Chauncey."

"Right," they told Rip again.

They continued to rock, sitting in silence on Rip's stylish flagstone patio, nodding their heads and playing games by placing their hands over their eyes and staring into the sun through the cracks between their fingers. "And how do we do that?" Willie said.

"Do what?"

"Get rid of Chauncey?"

"Well, it's very simple," said Rip, as he turned and smiled at his friends. "We kill him."

There was silence for a while, as Willie and Middlebaum stared at one another, but when they turned to look at Rip, they all three broke out laughing.

* * *

For a while, Willie had been able to forget about Middlebaum having to die, but Chauncey's sudden appearance abruptly changed things. Each minute Chauncey spent drinking and sleeping under the Beechwood Boulevard Bridge, was a minute stolen from their work on the dugout, which meant that a minute of joy might possibly be subtracted from Middlebaum's already abbreviated life.

Willie wished he could discuss his feelings about Middlebaum with someone else, most especially Rip. He wondered if Rip knew about Middlebaum dying. Mrs. Silver and Mrs. Middlebaum did not know each other, but Rip might have figured it out on his own somehow. As often as possible, when they were alone, Willie tried to bring Middlebaum up as a topic of conversation, but Rip always immediately changed the subject. Willie found Rip very difficult to understand. As the class "brain," why did he spend all of his free time with Middlebaum the freak and Willie the outcast?

With Rip out of the picture, Willie decided to talk to other people about Middlebaum. First, he made up his mind to tell Slippers, but when he finally found himself face-to-face with her, he couldn't concentrate on anything else but her bazoongies. Once, he went to talk to Rabbi Weiss, but the Rabbi was praying and couldn't be bothered. He headed over to visit Lenny Bernstein, but Lenny was practicing with his tuba. He stopped to see Kalson the grocer, Waldman the butcher, Mike the barber, but everybody was busy. In desperation, he wrote a letter to God.

> Dear God,
>   Why are you killing Ronald Middlebaum? And why must I be involved in this terrible murder? Why do I have to be the only one who knows that Middlebaum has to die? God is supposed to be good. He shouldn't go around killing people for no good reason. Unless they deserve it. But Ronald Middlebaum does not deserve it. He has had enough punishment. Please don't kill anybody. Please reconsider.
>
>   Affectionately,
>
>   Willie Heinemann

Willie folded the letter and put it into an envelope. He sealed the envelope and wrote "God" on the outside of it. Then he stooped down on the sidewalk in front of the synagogue, took out a book of matches, set fire to the envelope, and pushed the ashes into the gutter with his shoe.

God promptly answered Willie's letter late that night. As Willie lay sprawled red-eyed and alone on top of his bed, God said, *You can't stop death*. But then, Willie said to God, What should I do? And God, now leaning down and whispering into Willie's ear, said, *You can't stop death*. And Willie said, But what should I do? And God said, *You can't stop death*.

And Willie said.

And God said.

And the weeks went by.

Chapter VII
Chauncey Ruins Everything

Willie, Rip, and Middlebaum continued construction of the dug-out during those infrequent times when Chauncey wasn't there. Over the next couple of weeks, they worked maniacally, digging and dumping, two at a time, while the third member of the trio stood watch down on Beechwood Boulevard, waiting tensely for the coal man to come.

Twice, with Willie on guard, Chauncey sauntered unsteadily down the street, heading for the steps that led to the weeds that led to the bridge that led to them. Willie radioed the news to Middlebaum and Rip on his walkie-talkie, then scrambled back to warn them in person and to help them make their getaway. And although they continued to make progress, the simple and sorry fact of the matter was that the fun of the conception and shaping of Kiner's dugout was being soured by their fear of Chauncey. Something had to be done—and fast.

First, they tried writing letters:

"Dear Chauncey," (They penned the notes with their left hands, each boy alternating a word at a time.) "We understand you have relatives in Africa. For each day you are observed under the Beechwood Boulevard Bridge by our secret agents, one male member of your family will die." (signed) "Ramar of the Jungle."

"Dear Chauncey," said another, "The Beechwood Boulevard Bridge has been contaminated by Grabinski Weed. Grabinski Weed is most dangerous to colored people and to drunks. We calculate you only have five days to live. The only way to save yourself is to turn yourself in at the nearest police station." (signed) "The Pittsburgh Board of Agriculture."

"Listen Chauncey," said the last letter, "If you don't get out of town by tonight, we'll cut out your heart and make meat out of your feet." (signed) "Al Capone."

They placed the letters in a jar and put the jar in the dugout. Eventually, sometimes two or three days later, the letters were removed. Only once did they get a reply, scribbled in pencil on a scrap of brown paper bag.

> Dear Boys,
>   Please do not send me any more letters, as I have never been to school and cannot read.
>   Sincerely,
>   Chauncey

* * *

Now, weeks later, Wild Willie Hickock and Buffalo Middlebaum were at Rip's house. They squeaked back and forth on the glider, talking, watching while the night, like a big blackbird, swooped down on the town.

"Killing is a sin," said Willie.

"Having a rotten summer is also a sin," said Rip.

"Which is more of a sin?" asked Middlebaum.

"As sins go, killing is worse than having a rotten summer," said Rip. "On the other hand, three people are suffering if we have a rotten summer, but only Chauncey suffers if we kill him. The question is, 'Is killing three times more of a sin than having a rotten summer?' "

"Chauncey is also sinning by making us have a rotten summer," Willie pointed out. "The Bible says that anyone who sins should suffer."

Rip nodded. "The Bible says 'an eye for an eye.' "

"Tit for tat," Willie nodded.

"It says *that* in the Bible?" Middlebaum wanted to know.

"Meaning if you do something bad to a person, the person has the right to do something bad back to you," Rip explained.

"Chauncey's doing something bad to us."

"That's why we should kill him," said Rip.

Willie, Rip, and Middlebaum, still squeaking on the glider,

watched the fireflies dancing in the darkness, the scintilla of orange from the steel mills glowing in the sky.

"Well?" asked Rip.

"Well, what?"

"How should we do it?"

"Hang him," said Middlebaum. "Give him a trial, fair and square, convict him and hang him. It wouldn't be a sin. Slippers says every American deserves a fair trial."

"But for a trial we'll need a jury of 12 men and women. Nobody should know about this."

"I forgot."

"Besides, if we put Chauncey on trial, he might try to run away."

"Then we could shoot him. It's perfectly legal to shoot a man running away from a fair trial."

"Where would we get the gun?"

"Steal it from a policeman."

"Who would pull the trigger?"

Middlebaum looked at Rip, who looked at Willie, who looked back at Middlebaum.

"OK then, here's what we do," said Middlebaum. "We wait until we catch him sleeping, sneak up, and knife him in the back. My father's got plenty of knives; he's a butcher."

"Then maybe your father should kill Chauncey himself," Rip suggested. "Why should we get involved?"

"It'll never work. My father can't stand the sight of blood."

"I thought you said your father was a butcher."

Middlebaum shrugged. "He doesn't make much money."

"There are only two other alternatives," Rip announced. "Either we poison Chauncey or blow him up"

"We could easily get the poison at Kalson's by telling Mr. Kalson there's rats in our house."

"I don't think Mr. Kalson sells rat poisoning; there couldn't be any rats in Squirrel Hill. Rich people don't have rats. We should go to Greenfield. There are plenty of rats there," said Middlebaum.

"I've got it all worked out," said Willie. "We put the poison in a bottle of beer, wrap up the bottle in a box, real fancy with a ribbon and everything, and leave it in the dugout. Chauncey'll see the box and open it. He'll open the beer, too."

"What happens if he doesn't have an opener?"

"Drunks always carry openers with them. After all, drinking is their business."

"Then what?"

"Chauncey takes a big swig. The beer tastes good and he takes another big swig. Chauncey likes the beer so much he takes a third swig. You see what I mean?"

"What happens next?"

"Chauncey drops dead."

"What are we going to do with Chauncey's body?"

"Bury him."

"Forget it," said Middlebaum. "The whole thing would be a lot easier if we just blow him up with dynamite. He'll be scattered all over the place. We kill two birds with one stone. Not only is there no trace of Chauncey's body, but Chauncey is also dead."

Middlebaum wrinkled his brow and squinted his raisin eyes in thought before continuing. "We disguise the dynamite stick to look like a cigar, then see Chauncey on the street, go up and start talking. In the course of the conversation, we mention that our wife has just had a baby. 'Here Chauncey,' we say, 'we're celebrating. Have a cigar.' 'Thank you, boys,' he says. He puts the dynamite in his mouth and lights it. His face blows up."

"There's only one problem," said Rip. "Where are we going to get the dynamite?"

Middlebaum stamped his foot on the flagstone and shook his head. "Damn, nothing's going to work. We can't get the supplies we need."

"We could get gasoline," said Rip.

"We can't blow up Chauncey's face with gasoline."

"We could burn him to death."

"That's it," said Willie. "Burn Chauncey to death with gasoline."

"No one would suspect us," said Middlebaum. "If the police ever ask, Chauncey just caught on fire. That's all we know."

"The way I have it figured, the police would never connect us. It could all be an accident." Rip leaned forward, lowering his voice to a whisper, as he explained. "First we buy a gallon of gasoline, see? We put half the gas in each of two jars and wait for a time when Chauncey's under the bridge. Then me and Middlebaum get our jars of gasoline and take a walk. We're just walking casually, with our jars, you know? Nothing to attract attention to. We're not doing anything special. In the meantime, Willie is also taking a walk. And he happens to be smoking a cigarette. Willie arrives under the bridge with his burning cigarette about the same time we arrive with our jars of gasoline. Meanwhile, it just so happens that Chauncey is sleeping in the dugout." Rip paused to smile at Willie and Middlebaum who are leaning so far forward in their excitement that they are about ready to slip off the edge of the glider.

"Well, c'mon," said Middlebaum.

"You gonna make us wait all day?"

"I got this gasoline, and so does Middlebaum," Rip said. "Suddenly, I trip—accidentally. Then Middlebaum accidentally trips over me, and both our jars accidentally spill all over Chauncey. The gasoline wakes Chauncey up, but he's too stunned to know what's happening.

"At that exact same moment, Willie takes the final puff of his cigarette and flicks it into the nearest hole. That hole happens to have Chauncey in it, who just so happens to be drenched in gasoline. So Chauncey is ignited. He gets all burned up. We are innocent, don't even know what's happening. We just keep walking along, minding our own business, while Chauncey burns up behind us. We go home and go to sleep. The next day, we go down to the bridge and throw Chauncey's ashes on the street. The street cleaner comes around, sweeps up Chauncey's ashes and takes them to the city dump. The garbage men come and dump garbage on the ashes. Nobody will ever be able to recognize Chauncey's ashes mixed with the garbage. By the time anybody actually realizes Chauncey's gone, he'll be sprinkled all over the city dump. Possession is nine points of the law, and as long as nobody has possession of the ashes, we're free. It's the perfect plan."

Chapter VIII
The Arrival of God's Helicopter

Willie slithered through the window, dropped down into the dark cellar, and rummaged around until he discovered an old quilt. He doubled it over and spread it longways on the gray concrete floor. Next, he stuffed dirty shirts and underwear from his mother's laundry basket into a dirty pillowcase, and carried it to where he had spread out the quilt. Then he dropped down on the quilt, easing his head back onto the makeshift pillow.

It was very dark and cool in the cellar, and slowly his eyes began to close. Soon, he was stuffed into a pocket of darkness just as he had stuffed the dirty laundry into the pillowcase. The darkness was very heavy; he couldn't ignore it or push it away. It was a frightening experience, being awake enough to know he was asleep, but being too much asleep to manage to stay awake. Imprisoned by the sleep, he dreamed. He dreamed that he was sleeping and dreaming . . . he was dreaming that he was sleeping and dreaming . . . sleeping and dreaming. . . .

Willie boarded a banana boat in Brooklyn and cruised into a choppy blue sea. Willie's date was Abuzzi, and Middlebaum was with Slippers. The couples lulled away afternoons on colorful canvas deck chairs, watching the water and holding hands. At night, Abuzzi and Slippers took off all their clothes, from their black lace girdles to their ankle-strap, spike-heeled shoes, and danced around the room, their bazoongies dancing with them.

The steward was a black midget in a white uniform named Chauncey, who bowed to the men, curtsied to the women, and served them anything they wanted. The captain, who also wore a white uniform, was called Rip. Rip saluted everyone all the time. The six people went back and forth on their boat from Brooklyn to

Guatemala, and from Guatemala to Brooklyn, picking up and delivering bananas, but never stopping long enough to go ashore, because death was waiting for Ronald Middlebaum the moment he, or any of the others, touched ground.

As time passed, Abuzzi's stomach became very fat, and her bazoongies grew as large as basketballs, She hardly moved anymore, except to dance and eat, and she ate more than any man or woman Willie had ever known. She was the hungriest person on earth, devouring a turkey, a pot of beet borscht, a jello mold, and an entire strawberry cheesecake in one sitting. Meanwhile, this high living was also taking its toll on the beautiful Slippers, whose face was streaked red from too much wine, and whose eyes were ringed with spare tires. Her ass was now bigger than Jane Russell's; it was heading on toward Kate Smith country. But they all kept riding the waves from Brooklyn to Guatemala and back, picking up and delivering bananas, rocking and sleeping, drinking and dancing and eating, for what seemed like forever.

Middlebaum never died.

* * *

"So what did you do today?" Middlebaum asked, when they met later that afternoon.

"Nothing. I mean, I did something, but it really wasn't anything," said Willie.

"Don't you want to tell me?"

"I'd tell you if I thought you'd understand. I didn't even understand, and I did it."

"I'm your best friend, aren't I?"

"That doesn't mean you'd understand."

"It means I have a right to know."

"Well, I was sleeping."

"Were you sick?"

"No, I was in the cellar."

"I thought you said you were sleeping."

"I told you, you wouldn't understand."

"Because you're not explaining, is why I don't understand."

"I just got up in the morning and went down the cellar, and

before I even knew what I was doing, I was sleeping."

"But in the cellar?"

"I didn't want to see anybody. I wanted to be alone, and I wanted to be in the dark." Willie wrinkled his nose in puzzlement. "I don't understand it myself. It was queer," he said.

"Probably you were tired," Middlebaum said.

"I wasn't tired. I can hardly sleep at night, and if I was tired I would go to sleep then. That's when you're supposed to sleep."

"Why don't you go to sleep at night like everybody else?"

Willie shrugged. "I don't like closing my eyes because then I can't see what's happening."

"What could happen?"

"I could be ambushed by Zeewee, for one thing—or my ulcer. It's safer all around with my eyes open," Willie said. "I guess I'm a chicken."

"You're no chicken," Middlebaum told him. "Just because you might feel afraid doesn't make you a chicken. As long as you don't run away. You always gotta stay and fight. Just so you don't run away, that's the thing."

"Sleeping, especially in the cellar, is running away," Willie pointed out.

"The guys in the war," Middlebaum said, ignoring Willie, "they were afraid of the Japs and Nazis, but no American actually ran away."

"Plenty ran away," Willie said. He did not think that was true, but he said it anyway.

"Well, I never met any of them or read about them."

"Deserters were everywhere," Willie said. "There were millions."

"Our fathers didn't run away; *they* fought the Nazis."

"My father was a cook in the war. He learned how to make spaghetti sauce."

"It was just as dangerous to be a cook as it was to be fighting on the front lines because the Nazis had V-2 death rockets," said Middlebaum. "They could hit you anywhere they wanted. They blew up kitchens by zeroing-in on pots and pans. The guys in the war, fighting the Nazis, were probably afraid, I'll admit to that, but most didn't run away. That's the difference, you see," Middlebaum insisted, wagging his finger, "it's the running away I'm complaining about."

As Willie listened, he realized that Middlebaum was trying to work up enough courage to say something important—something that Willie knew instinctively he did not want to hear. Willie liked being close to a person, having a friend with enough confidence in their relationship to tell him personal things. But that didn't mean he wanted to *know* anything personal; he just wanted to be eligible to find out. He wanted to be considered trustworthy, but didn't want to be trusted. So, to avoid the discussion, he said, "Sometimes it's easier to be brave than chicken. I mean, it would have been harder for the GIs in World War II to run away from the Nazis than to fight them. For one thing, anywhere the GIs went, there were Nazi spies and Nazi bombs and Jap kamikaze pilots. There was no escape. They were trapped. The GIs had to fight one way or another. Maybe they didn't want to fight," Willie rambled, "but they had to fight . . ."

"Look," Middlebaum interrupted, "sometimes when I'm supposed to go to the doctor's office, I don't get there. I tell my mother I'm there, but I never really go . . ."

"Let's go play football," Willie said. "Let's get an ice cream cone. Let's visit Zeewee."

But Middlebaum was determined. He was all red-faced, and his raisin eyes were glittering in their sockets like beetles' backs. "Sometimes when I'm supposed to go to the doctor's, I just walk around the streets or sit in a drug store and drink Cokes. This afternoon I was supposed to be at the doctor's. I almost got there. I made it as far as the elevator before I chickened out. Sometimes I make it all the way to the bathroom next door to his office before I run away. It's terrible. All the doctor does when I'm there is examine me. He never hurts me. He just shuts off the light, lays me down on a cool steel table and examines my nose and throat, takes some pictures. That's all there is to it."

Willie couldn't listen anymore. He didn't know or care what he was saying, but found himself talking as loud and fast as possible. "Maybe, just maybe, it was easier for the GIs to fight. That's all I can think of. Maybe, in fact, they chickened out by facing the Nazis and fighting. That's what they did all right. Sure, now I know," Willie said.

"Sometimes he sticks me with a needle, puts this needle as long as my arm into my ear. I wanna bleed all over his coat, the bastard, the bastard! But I can't squeeze a drop of blood out of my ear. I push with all of my might, but there's no goddam blood. And it doesn't hurt; nothing hurts. I can't feel anything. Even when I try to feel, I can't feel. I'm immune to physical feeling. It's as if my skin is all made of rubber."

"There's no doubt about it," Willie said. "They were afraid to run away, so they fought. Fighting the Nazis face-to-face was the chicken's way out. If they were really brave, they would have retreated . . ." Willie was determined to keep on talking, but right at that very moment, God turned up the volume of Middlebaum's voice and simultaneously shut Willie off completely. As hard as he tried, Willie suddenly could not speak, could no longer even move his mouth to interrupt.

"It's just how they look at me when I go to the doctor's office that bothers me most of all," Middlebaum said. "They're treating me too nice, like I'm someone special. But I'm only Ronald Middlebaum, and they have no right treating me so good. That's the thing. I'm no big deal. And so, sometimes I don't go. Then the nurse calls up my mother and reports me. My mother gets mad, screams and hollers, and drags me to the doctor's anyway. But I don't care. It doesn't make any difference. She can drag me to the doctor's all she wants. She can drag me until I'm dragged to death as far as I'm concerned. But I'm not going to go on my own, by myself—not until they stop treating me so good. Something's wrong somewhere when they treat me so good. They have no right."

Middlebaum was breathing very hard now. The ping pong ball vibrated wildly. His underarms were soaking wet. "Look at you," his finger shot out at Willie. "You have an ulcer and that's pretty serious, but do you go to the doctor's all the time? You hardly ever go. And when you do go, the doctor is mean and makes you wait. And he pokes you in the stomach, and you have to drink liquid chalk for the X-ray machine. So why not me? That's what I want to know. That's what I don't understand. Why do I have to go to the doctor's so often, and when I'm there, why does he treat me so nice?"

Inside himself Willie was a shambles as he stared up at the tall narrow splinter of a soon-to-be-dead person that was his friend. Up to this very second, there had always been a vague sliver of doubt that Middlebaum was going to die. There was always the chance that Willie's parents could have been wrong, and that Middlebaum was actually perfectly all right. Even if his parents had been right, Middlebaum could still manage to pull through by some quirk of fate. But Willie's hope for Ronald Middlebaum's survival disappeared when he heard the faraway sound of God's helicopter.

He heard it beating from a long way off, sharp and dull at the same time, thudding like a lumberjack's chopping axe. It was coming on quickly. The sound was growing louder and faster, CLOPPCLOPPCLOPP, THUDTHUD, creating a terrible vibrating racket, CLOPPCLOPPCLOPPCLOPP. Then suddenly it came into view, bursting out of the clouds, swooping down into the neighborhood and situating itself directly over Middlebaum's head. This was the biggest and loudest machine Willie had ever seen or heard. Willie could see or hear nothing else in the whole world now but God and His helicopter.

And yet, Ronald Middlebaum did not hear it. He just stood there, hands on hips, staring at Willie. And he was crying. Willie had never seen Middlebaum cry before. Even when Zeewee and Kenner picked on him, Middlebaum always managed not to cry.

Willie caught a glimpse of God sitting inside the helicopter in a red velvet cockpit throne, dressed in a white robe with a white beard and white buck shoes. Willie took out his walkie-talkie and radioed up to Him. "Get out of here. What do you want from us? Get out of here. Over."

God shrugged His shoulders, put on His earphones and plugged the radio jack into the control panel. "Don't you see? There's nothing I can do about this. Over."

Without another word, God and His helicopter dissolved into the sky.

Middlebaum was silent and Willie was silent, and the sky was silent now as they started to walk. Middlebaum's tears had disappeared as quickly as they had come. The sun was orange, licking the tips of distant houses. A vague early moon hung below the clouds.

Though things were happening all around him—cars passing and honking, people waving and laughing—it was so quiet, Willie could hear his whole body work. He could hear the mucous in his chest whistling as air passed through, the engine in his heart pumping, shooting blood that rolled like a bowling ball down an alley, just rolling and rolling, down alley after alley, without ever pounding the pins. He could hear Middlebaum's tennis shoes squeak in the moist grass, crunch in the gravel, scrape against cement. He could hear Middlebaum talking. And it was as if

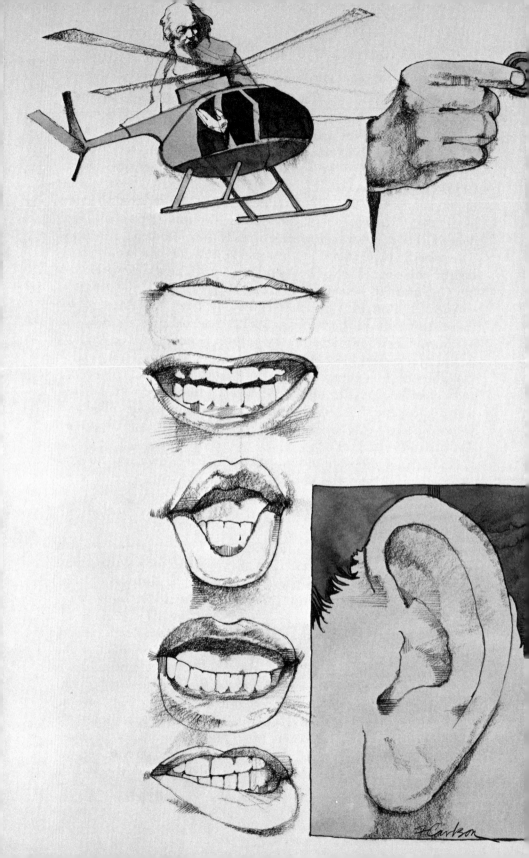

Middlebaum's voice was hooked to a loud speaker system, that he was actually talking into a microphone, that the microphone was located in a long, tight, steel tunnel, that the end of the tunnel was slanted to a point with the opening big enough for Willie's ear, that Willie's ear was locked right into the opening, so that no matter how loud Middlebaum said it, and how much the sound was magnified, Willie would be the only one listening. Middlebaum's words were recorded and played back a dozen times. And each time it was played, God turned the volume up louder, louder than the atomic bomb blast, louder than Willie's father screaming at him from the bathroom; it got louder and louder, ever louder as it played:

"PRETTY SOON I'VE GOT TO HAVE AN OPERATION. PRETTY SOON I'VE GOT TO HAVE AN OPERATION."

Willie listened to each word carefully, to the whole sentence, to little phrases that made up the sentence—PRETTY SOON. I'VE GOT. TO HAVE. AN OPERATION—until God's helicopter once again returned.

Willie first heard the thumping, then almost immediately saw it, moving fast over the soon-to-be-night sky. The helicopter hovered above them, and Willie saw God in His cockpit clearly. There was a button in God's hand which Willie immediately recognized as coming from Middlebaum's pea jacket. When God pressed the button, a cannon emerged from the bottom of the helicopter. The cannon had a rocket inside it.

Suddenly, there was a puff of smoke, followed by a small explosion, and Willie saw the rocket zooming straight as an arrow toward them. It looked like a shooting star with its tail of fire as it sliced through the sky, but it actually was a Nazi V-2 death rocket sent to destroy them.

Luckily, however, it hadn't been aimed very well, for it veered off across the street and up a hill, detonating harmlessly in a vacant lot. The explosion seemed deafening, although Middlebaum clearly hadn't seen or heard anything that had taken place.

When Willie was sure he and Middlebaum were safe, he let out a long sigh of relief and smiled triumphantly at God. God smiled back at Willie, pressed the pea jacket button which deactivated the cannon. Willie could hear God laughing as He chopped away.

"When's it going to be? When you gonna have the operation?" Willie asked.

"They're waiting a month and a half until school lets out, but it also has to do with a doctor who's coming from New York, a specialist. We don't know when he's going to arrive."

"Specialists are foolproof," Willie assured him. "A specialist loses his license if even one operation fails."

Chapter IX
Rubbing Chauncey Out

Why did God want to kill Ronald Middlebaum, and what was waiting for Ronald Middlebaum once he was dead? A partial answer came a few days later while Willie was spending one of his increasingly frequent afternoons in his basement bed.

He realized that being down in the basement was very much like being dead. Willie was entombed under his house just like Middlebaum would be entombed under a gray stone marker, and Willie could look out the cellar window and see the world happening all around him. He could hear voices, smell the dust of the basement and the dirty clothes, listen to the water heater click on and off. From the cellar window, Willie could see, understand, and relate to almost everything surrounding his tomb. He could watch the neighbors. He could imagine anything he desired. He could walk up to Zeewee and smash him in the chin. And although Zeewee didn't know it, when Willie hit him, he would tumble down out cold or dead, whatever Willie happened to conjure up. Willie was all-powerful. As long as he stayed in the graveyard under his house, he could go anywhere, do anything, be anyone. He would marry Slippers or Abuzzi, become President of the United States or General of the Army of the Pacific. Willie was wise, strong, handsome, and charming. Girls loved Willie in the basement. As long as he remained entombed, he was free to choose his own life and to live it to the hilt. As long as he remained in the basement, he was entitled to life, liberty, and friendship with Kiner, God, or Ronald Middlebaum.

But if he attempted to escape, to participate in life, he would be through. He could never try to break out of the basement because, if he failed, then he would truly be a prisoner. As long as he lived from the inside and locked his brain in the basement, he would be free. That must be the difference between life and death; there could be no other answer. Death was living on the inside, like living in a basement. And, if Middlebaum was heading for this kind of end, well, perhaps it wasn't an end after all. Death was only a physical thing, anyway. How can you kill your own head? Unless they are burned or crushed, your eyes will see, your ears will hear, your tastebuds will tingle. Even if somebody put a bullet in your brain, your ability to think and dream would be there. Nothing could stop that. There were millions upon trillions upon quadrillions of minds roaming around the world. Pig's minds, dog's minds, elephant's minds, people's minds. They congregated somewhere and communicated somehow, that's how it must be.

Willie realized the necessity of getting the dugout finished. It was not only for Middlebaum's or Willie's sake, but for the two of them together. It was essential to have a private place available, a place they could share, a place where they could meet in secrecy after Middlebaum was dead.

*   *   *

From his mother, Middlebaum stole some Lucky Strike cigarettes which Willie wrapped in wax paper to preserve. Instead of gasoline they filled two quart-sized pickle jars with turpentine Willie's father kept in the basement to clean paint brushes, then stored the cigarettes and the jars in the bushes under the steps leading to the bridge. They did this Friday afternoon, then went home, had dinner, watched TV. Middlebaum picked Willie up, then they called on Rip. By 7:30 p.m. all three boys were at the foot of the bridge, the plan of assassination clear in their minds.

"What if we're caught?" Middlebaum asked.

First, they'd be fugitives from justice, Rip explained, men who wear masks, rob from the rich in Squirrel Hill to give to the poor and who, when captured, could be plugged into an electric chair or hanged by the neck on national TV until the Governor commuted their sentences. Either way, they would undoubtedly be heroes, especially when they explained that Chauncey's real name was CHAUN-CEE, a North Korean soldier, scouting in advance of an enemy attack.

As Rip talked, he handed out the equipment, cigarette and matches for Willie, jars of turpentine to Middlebaum and himself. He stood up and turned to Middlebaum. "Take the lid off your jar."

"What for?"

"Because then we're committed," said Rip. "We won't back down so quickly if we aren't able to close up the jars. Otherwise, it would be too easy to chicken out." Without another word, Rip unscrewed the lid of the jar and tossed it into the weeds. Middlebaum hesitated momentarily, then followed suit.

This was very serious now, far more serious and ominous than Willie had expected. Feeling like his knees had suddenly been rubberized and a balloon was inflating his belly, Willie led them slowly up the concrete steps.

They could see the yellow of Chauncey's campfire flickering under the bridge. There was also a moon hanging silver-gray in the sky and blue and red and yellow stars twinkling. Willie gained confidence as his eyes adjusted to the darkness. Middlebaum and Rip were close behind him. He could hear the thunder of their breathing in the scary silence. Halfway between Beechwood Boulevard below and Murray Avenue above, they ducked under the cold iron railing and plunged into the damp darkness of the weeds. God had dropped dew everywhere, cold and oily as they walked. Branches slapped their faces, bushes soaked their clothes. But they pressed on. Willie could smell Chauncey's campfire, homey and comfortable. He could detect the odor of Chauncey, whiskey and smelly feet.

Soon Willie, Rip, and Middlebaum crept to the edge of the clearing. They saw the yellow of the fire flickering from inside the dugout, but there seemed to be no one around it. No one was leaning against the wall, no one was strolling nearby. There were no sentries or armed guards or unsuspecting settlers. No one seemed to be there. They stood up, taking one and then another cautious step toward the light of the fire. Where the hell was Chauncey?

"He's not here," whispered Middlebaum.

"He's here somewhere," said Rip.

"Maybe it's an ambush," Willie suggested, reaching instinctively down to the holster side of his pants to where he wished his six-shooter was.

"I spilled half of the turpentine crawling through the bushes," whispered Middlebaum.

"You still have plenty," said Rip.

Willie unwrapped the waxpaper and put the Lucky Strike between his lips. "Are you ready?" he said.

"Ready," said Rip.

"Yeah," said Middlebaum.

Willie lighted his cigarette. He took a few puffs, then began walking across the clearing, but as far away from the dugout as possible. On the way, he met Middlebaum and Rip, who were also out strolling. "Good evening, Mr. Middlebaum," said Willie. "And howdy-do to you, Rip."

"Good evening, Willie," said Rip, doffing his imaginary hat.

"My good man," Middlebaum said, nodding.

Now they were on opposite sides of the clearing, but still no Chauncey. Willie tried to be as casual as possible as he took a few more puffs and strode carefully back across the clearing, angling a bit nearer to the dugout. "Nice night," he said off-handedly as Rip and Middlebaum just happened to walk by.

"Indeed it is, sir," said Rip, once again doffing his hat.

"Ideal for a stroll," said Middlebaum.

Back at the edge of the clearing where he started, Willie saw he only had a few more puffs on his cigarette remaining, so he decided to take a walk to the corner drug store to get a new pack. On his way, he happened to run into a couple of old friends. "Well, well, well, if it isn't old Middlebaum and old Rip," said Willie.

"Well, well, well, if it isn't our friend Willie," said Middlebaum and Rip as they walked casually by.

So there was Middlebaum, and there was Rip, and there was Chauncey's fire flickering in the dugout, but still no Chauncey. There was only one other place he could be. From opposite edges of the clearing, they all stared at the hole in the ground that was eventually going to be Kiner's home away from home. Then Willie and Rip and Middlebaum got themselves poised and set.

"Well, Mr. Middlebaum, it certainly was nice of you to accompany me on this stroll, but I think I'll head on home," Rip said. "I have many things to do, you know, I'm a busy man."

"Yes, indeed, I think I'll join you," said Middlebaum.

"But first I must get rid of this jar of trash I picked up. I can't stand litter, even if it is liquid."

"I, too," said Middlebaum, very loudly, facing the dugout. "Litter is lousy."

"This cigarette butt must go as well," said Willie. "But where shall we put all this junk?"

"Hark," said Rip. "Is that a hole in the ground over yonder, no doubt dug for this very purpose by the Department of Sanitation and Garbage?"

"Indeed, indeed," said Middlebaum.

From opposite sides of the clearing, Willie, Rip and Middlebaum took a hesitant step toward the dugout. They stopped, then started, creeping forward slowly, toe and heel, as if they were testing the strength of the ground before trusting it with their weight. Now Willie's knees were quaking, and his heart beat like an Indian war drum. They stopped and started until they worked their way right up to the edge of the dugout. Simultaneously, they stared down inside.

In his mind, Willie started to run. He ran as far as the Cleveland bus station, hopped a Greyhound, and drove it at 400 mph toward San Antonio, Texas. But, in reality, Willie's feet could not move. Neither could the feet of Rip and Middlebaum. They stood there for a long time, for seconds as long as hours and minutes which lasted half the night, their brains unwilling to accept what they all along knew to be true. For leaning back against the wall of the dugout in Kiner's honored place was Chauncey, his wrinkled bronze face reflecting fire and night.

Chapter X
Chauncey Tells His Tale

"What you got in them jars?" Chauncey demanded.

Willie, Rip, and Middlebaum were so scared at that moment, that they could only muster enough strength to take an imaginary step backward.

"What you got in them jars?" Chauncey said again. His voice was harsh and raspy, somehow not fully intact, as if he had lost part of a vocal cord somewhere. He reached into his jacket pocket, pulled out a bottle, tilted his head back, and drank from it. Then he leaned forward: "Now what you got in them jars?"

"Ww, ww, whiskey," Willie stammered.

"Ha, whiskey! Whiskey!" shrieked Chauncey, cracking open his black face to reveal a piano key grin. "Son, you take them jars and set 'em down over there by the edge of the clearing."

"You want a drink?" Middlebaum offered.

"You want to join me?" asked Chauncey.

Willie snatched the jars and dumped them into the weeds.

"Now, you just sit yourselfs down, all three of you, and we'll talk," Chauncey said when Willie returned. "It's been a long time since I done got the chance to talk to such fine young men."

The boys remained standing, but Chauncey didn't seem to notice. "Chilly tonight," he said, leaning forward, rubbing his hands together, dipping his fingers into the flames.

"Aren't you afraid of getting burned?" Willie asked.

"From this here fire? Son, you don't know nothin', do you?" He thrust out his hand. "Feel."

Obediently, Willie and Rip reached out and touched Chauncey's hand. So did Middlebaum. They had never before touched skin that was any other color but white.

"Well?" Chauncey asked.

"It feels like sandpaper," Middlebaum said.

"It looks like tree bark," Rip noted.

Chauncey shook his head, raised his eyebrow, and let out a long, deep hissing sigh of disapproval. "Boys, from head to toe my skin is made with the one substance in America guaranteed not to burn."

Willie, Rip, and Middlebaum looked at one another, smiling from ear-to-ear in relief as they gathered around Chauncey and sat down beside him.

After all, anyone who knew the secret of asbestos just had to be a friend.

"What were you doing in our dugout?" Middlebaum said, after they had properly introduced themselves, shook hands all around like grown-ups. "We dug that hole by ourselves. It's our head-quarters building."

"It's a memorial," said Willie, "to the greatest living American in the United States."

"Ralph Kiner, the slugging, homerun-hitting left fielder of the Pittsburgh Pirates. You see this jacket?" said Rip, fingering his ripped sleeve, while Willie and Middlebaum looked on respectfully. "This was once Kiner's jacket until he threw it out."

"Well, boys," Chauncey said, nodding, "that's real impressive, but this here place ain't no memorial to Ralph Kiner or to anyone else. This here's my home. I been here off and on since nineteen hundred and twenty-nine. That's a long time ago, nineteen and twenty-nine, and I goin' to be here until the day I die. You boys are in my home."

"But this is only a hole under a bridge," Middlebaum protested. "This isn't a home. A home is a house or an apartment where there's a bed and a kitchen and a bathroom."

Chauncey rubbed a tree bark hand over his wrinkled face. "Relax, boys, lean back and make yourselfs comfortable. Ain't no reason to be so upset. This here's my home." He paused and looked at them with fire-reflecting eyes. "You go to school, do you?"

They nodded.

"No wonder you so damn stupid." Chauncey shook his head, raised a brow, and hissed his disapproving sneer. "You learn from books? If that's all you learning from, then you ain't learning nothin'."

"We learn history," Rip said, maintaining his loyalty to Slippers and Herbert Hoover, "and science and hygiene."

"If that's all you learning, then you ain't learning nothin'." Chauncey pulled out his whiskey, uncapped and poured amber liquid down his throat, wiped his mouth with a ragged sleeve.

"We also learn arithmetic, spelling, and geography."

"You still ain't learning nothin'. A man's got to live to learn, the way I sees it, and goin' to school ain't living. That's how the people who learning you done learned, and they ain't lived no-how. They learned the same way as you, by sitting and talking, which ain't living, so it ain't learning."

Willie jabbed Middlebaum in the side with his elbow. "Our teacher has probably *lived* more than anybody."

"She's probably 'lived' you under the table," said Rip.

"She's a blonde bombshell," said Middlebaum. "Like Lana Turner."

"Some dish, eh boys?" Chauncey smiled, stood up, and started to pace slowly around the dugout. His legs were much shorter than his pants, and he dragged his tattered cuffs behind him.

"Now you boys say a home ain't a home unless you got a roof and a refrigerator. So that's what you say?" he asked, pausing to lift his brow, and hiss and sneer disapprovingly. "Well, it ain't your fault you're so damn dumb, because that's what they teached you in school, and in them books. But let me tell you this. There's a big difference between a place you eat in and sleep in and another place you call home."

Chauncey groped in his jacket pocket, took out his whiskey bottle and stared at it, as he continued to pace around the dugout. "Now, sometimes I sleep and eat in my brother's home. He's a janitor in the apartment house up the street. Ha! My brother is my keeper. But it ain't my home. It ain't even his home. Ha! He wishes down deep he was out with me drinking and running around, 'stead of being around his nagging wife, although he don't often admit it. 'Cause boys, here, under this bridge, is peace and quiet and freedom. Here is a home. There, with his nagging wife, is nothin' but a place to sit and eat and sleep and work. That ain't no home. It ain't no home unless you happy working, and there ain't no black man can be happy cleaning and fixing for white people, which is what my brother goin' to be doin' for the rest of his life."

Chauncey paused to take a big swallow from his bottle; his shoulders shook as the whiskey went down. "Now I come up here from North Caroline in 1925," he said, starting to pace around once more. "I *walked* up here from North Caroline 'stead of taking a bus or train 'cause all I got is money for food, and there weren't no white man goin' to pick up this here nigger on the road and drive him north, no matter how prosperous he be looking." Chauncey stopped. He seemed to stop his pacing at the end of a sentence and start it up each time he began a new one. "And I was looking pretty prosperous back then, if I do say so myself, wearing one brand new suit I just bought, and carrying a second never worn in a cardboard box. 'Course, I tried to hitchhike everyday, cars passing, but me not getting one lousy ride, new suit and all."

Willie, Rip, and Middlebaum leaned forward, watching Chauncey talk and walk. Decorated with reflections from the flickering fire, his steady pacing made him seem nearly hypnotic.

"Takes me two, three weeks," Chauncey continued, "sleeping out in the cold and trudging through the rain, but I get to Pittsburgh and right away look up my brother, who is working on this here bridge. THIS BRIDGE." Chauncey jumped up and down on his pantcuffs, pounding in the point.

"My brother, he got friends all over, especially with the white man, since he's so much of a hard worker. So he goes up to the foreman and points to me and says, 'That there's my brother, and he's just as much a hard worker as me, so howsabout giving him a job, too?' "

Willie felt entranced, as if he were watching an especially exciting episode of Captain Video on television.

"So the foreman, he look me up and down, backwards and forwards, and asks to feel my muscle. He takes a good long look at my shoes, to see if they is in good enough shape. And then, before you know it, I'm working on this bridge, as easy as that."

Chauncey rolled his eyes and wrinkled his brows, thinking hard and remembering, as he squinted far back into his past.

"This was the happiest time in my life, boys, working for two years straight. Sundays off. Sometimes loading wheelbarrows and sometimes pushing wheelbarrows when someone else is loading.

Money in my pocket. Pretty young girls at my side. Goin' to dances Saturday nights. Having a room of my own in a boarding house with a window facing the street. My brother, he quits after a while and goes to work for another construction company, which is building an apartment house, but I'm too happy working on this bridge. I ain't got nothin' against apartment houses, but this bridge, you see, was a wonderful thing. For the first time in my life, I felt like I was making a contribution to something. This bridge was for all the people, while the apartment house being built was just for the benefit of the man who collect the rent. My brother was smart. He didn't care about contributions. He more concerned with survival. He knows that this bridge ain't goin' to take forever to be built. He told me more than once, but I still don't want to leave. Well, pretty soon, the bridge is done, just as he warned. The stock market crashes, people are jumping out of windows, the Depression is coming around the corner, and I ain't got no job.

"No job," Chauncey repeated, raising his head, eyes skyward. "No money," he said, lowering head. "No dances," raising his head. "No girls. It was as fast as that. First I is in clover, and then I is in mud."

He drew his shoulders up and into his chin and shrugged. "Well, I just floated around for a while. I got nowhere to go, nothin' to do, and no one to care for, or to care for me. And you see, boys," said Chauncey, finally sitting back down on the edge of the dugout, dangling his feet inside, "that's the secret of life. You got to have somebody to take care of you. You got to have somebody to love." Chauncey dropped his head until his chin touched his chest.

Willie knew what Chauncey meant. Life was nothing without someone to be with, someone you like. He glanced at Middlebaum.

"Well, you can't blame your brother," said Rip. "He knew how and when to plan for the future."

"That's what we're doing now," Middlebaum said. "We're planning ahead so that we'll have a good summer."

But Chauncey wasn't listening. Still staring out into the night, he drank some more whiskey and wiped his lips with his sleeve. "I went some places, did some things, met some people after that," he said.

"And then what?" Middlebaum wanted to know.

"Then I died," said Chauncey. "Leastways, I was good as dead."

"What?"

"I go to sleep in 1934 a young man. I wake up in 1949 and I is old, boys, like a dried-out turd." Although there were no tears in his black and yellow eyes, Chauncey's face sobbed in silence.

"Then one day, not too many years ago, I comes across this here bridge again. I ain't thought about this bridge for a lot of years, but suddenly, this here little voice inside of me says, 'Chauncey, you back home.' Well, I ain't had a home nowheres since. I slept some other places, lots of other places, but I ain't never had a home nowhere else since."

"That's like us," Middlebaum said. "We sleep and eat in our parents' houses, but this is our home."

"But this is *my* home," said Chauncey. "I got squatter's rights. I was here first. This here's my home."

"But we're here a lot," said Rip, "and you're hardly ever here. I mean, there's no sign of you living here."

"This is my home," said Chauncey. "You got to clean your home real well every day to make it nice, ain't that right?"

The boys nodded and everyone was silent for a while listening to the cars whoosh by on the street below. Chauncey, fanning the coals with his hand, dropped some more wood on the fire.

"What did you do from 1934 to 1949?" Rip asked.

"I told you," Chauncey answered flatly, "I died."

"We're not stupid. A person can't be dead and alive at the same time."

"Dead is forever," said Willie, who considered himself an expert on death. "Dead is dead."

"I was not only dead, but buried," Chauncey said.

"Where?" asked Middlebaum.

"In the graveyard of the living," Chauncey replied, "known as the Allegheny County Jail."

At first, there was a stunned silence as the impact of Chauncey's shattering announcement set in. "An *ex-con*," Middlebaum marveled. "All my life I've wanted to meet an *ex-con*."

"I thought they only let *ex-cons* out of jail long enough to make movies," said Willie.

"Are you *going straight?*" asked Rip.

"Are you making a movie?" said Willie.

"They got him on a *bum rap*," Middlebaum giggled.

Willie and Rip and Middlebaum were laughing and squirming and bouncing up and down. "You were *framed*, I'll bet," Middlebaum

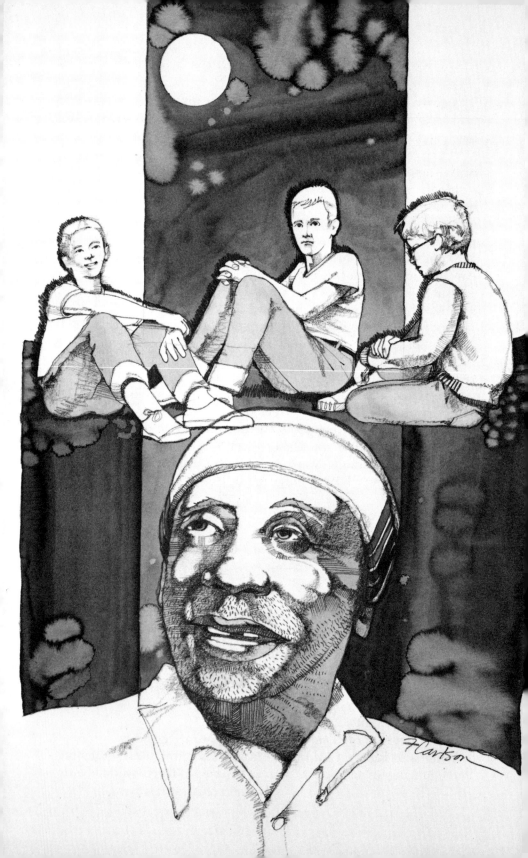

yelled, the ping pong ball ricocheting, "Chauncey was *framed.*"

"A bum rap."

"For burglary."

"Kidnapping," said Middlebaum.

"No, it was bankrobbing. Chauncey knocked over a bank and got away with a million dollars."

"And buried it under this bridge!"

Now they were up on their feet, dancing around Chauncey like Indians. "Chauncey knocked over a bank, he knocked over a bank, he stole money," they sang.

"No, boys," Chauncey said, smiling and shaking his head. "You got me all wrong. You see, I'm a murderer."

Middlebaum, Willie, and Rip stopped their dancing and prancing and yelling and dropped in their tracks. A bank robber was one thing, a murderer another. Would they get out from under the bridge alive? Or would they be massacred at dawn?

"I killed a man," Chauncey told them.

Willie could see the flash of lights from the cars driving under the bridge below. There weren't nearly as many going by now as there were when they first came up those 26 steps an hour or two hours or maybe even three hours ago. He hoped that the late hour, the excitement, and now the fright of sitting face-to-face with a real murderer wasn't too much for the weak heart of Ronald Middlebaum to take.

After a good long time of staring at the fire, Chauncey, grim and serious, said: "I ain't going to hurt you boys, so relax. You see, you were right."

Middlebaum, Rip and Willie sighed. "You mean you were framed?"

"Oh, I done murdered the man, killed him on the spot. I surely did that. But it was in self-defense."

"I knew it," Middlebaum stared across the fire in admiration.

"Nobody done believed it," said Chauncey. "But sure as I'm sitting here, it was self-defense."

"Not many guys get a chance to kill somebody in self-defense," said Middlebaum.

"It was during the Depression," said Chauncey, staring down at the fire. "Ain't no money or jobs for nobody back then. The whole world's starving."

"My mother raised chickens in her back yard to stay alive during the Depression," said Willie. "My Uncle Herbie went to the Salvation Army each afternoon and stood in line to eat soup."

"A bad time for most everybody," said Chauncey. "But me? For once I gets lucky. A man who owns a grocery store gave me some meals in return for me washing his windows and sweeping his floors. I did that for three months, washing and wiping; I never starved once. Then, one morning—it was in the spring, right about this time of year, as I recall—while I'm sweeping, he says he's got to go down the street to collect a bill, but if anybody comes into the store to tell them to wait 'cause he'll be right back."

Just then, Chauncey discovered an imaginary broom in his hands. Immediately, he began impersonating himself, sweeping up the dirt.

"After a few minutes, a white man starts to watch me through the window. He was a big fella," said Chauncey, as he swept the imaginary dirt into a neat pile, "as tall as this here jasper." He pointed at Middlebaum.

"'Mr. Frederick will be right back,' I holler at him through the glass.

"Well, he watches me without saying anything, just picking his teeth with a toothpick and watching. Then he throws the toothpick down and comes inside. 'Open up the cash register,' he says."

Chauncey leaned on his imaginary broom and shook his head. "'I can't,' I told him, 'it's locked.'"

Chauncey's broom disappeared. He shoved his hand deep into his jacket pocket and then pulled it out of the pocket. His thumb and forefinger were now shaped like a gun.

"'Open up the cash register,' the white man says again, 'or I'll plug you.'"

The gun disappeared and the broom instantly reappeared. Chauncey's voice quivered. "'But I ain't got the key.'"

Suddenly, Middlebaum jumped to his feet and strode right up to Chauncey, face-to-face. A gun appeared in Middlebaum's hand. A scowl creased his cheeks. "If you don't give me the money, I'll shoot," Middlebaum drawled like an outlaw.

For an instant, Chauncey was caught by surprise, but he recovered quickly. He turned to Willie and Rip who were staring in amazement, never having witnessed a real-life robbery before, especially with Middlebaum participating.

"Then I knocked the gun out of his hand and kicked it over into the corner," said Chauncey. "I fell on top of him before he could grab it."

Middlebaum dropped to his knees, and Chauncey jumped on top of him.

"First, I gets the best of him," Chauncey narrated. "Then he gets the best of me."

Middlebaum rolled on top of Chauncey.

"But I struggle to my feet, fighting tooth and nail," Chauncey said from under Middlebaum.

Chauncey and Middlebaum struggled to their feet, splattering each other—*bam-bam-bam*—with make-believe punches.

Watching carefully, Willie didn't know what to think. He wanted Middlebaum to win the fight, but wanted Chauncey to beat the hell out of the crook who got him framed.

"Finally," said Chauncey, "I remember the knife I keep in my pocket for just such occasions."

Suddenly, there appeared a make-believe Bowie knife as long as Chauncey's arm.

"I raise up my shiv," Chauncey said lunging forward. "And I plunge it into the white bastard's belly."

Middlebaum gasped, clutched his stomach, sank to his knees, tumbled over head first, moaned four times, quivered twice, and died in the dust.

In the few seconds that it took for the truth of what he had just seen to sink into his brain and connect with his heart, Willie got very upset. So did Middlebaum, standing up and brushing dirt from his clothes, and Rip as well.

"You got sent to jail for that?" Rip said.

"Sure as I'm sitting here."

"But that was self-defense. What did your lawyer say to the judge and jury?"

"He say the truth."

"What did the jury say?"

"They say guilty to the second degree."

"What did the judge say?" Willie wanted to know.

"He say fifteen years."

"Did you get paroled?"

"Parole for white people only."

"They can't get away with that," said Rip. "You're a victim of injustice. This is America. There's no injustice in America."

"Well, they got away with it, sure as I'm sittin' here."

"Who did this to you?" said Willie. His nose had suddenly stuffed up. Moisture was coming from his eyes and rolling down his cheeks.

"People," Chauncey shrugged.

"I hate people," said Middlebaum, he too sniffing, tears coating his face.

"People are lousy," said Rip, pulling his handkerchief out of his front pocket, blowing his nose, and stuffing the handkerchief back inside.

"There's smoke in my eyes," Willie said.

"It wasn't so bad," said Chauncey. "In jail they give you a bed and three meals a day. I made a lot of friends there, too, although they all dead now. Now I ain't got no friends."

"My asthma is acting up," said Middlebaum, "and my sinuses are leaking." He wiped his face with a dusty shirt tail.

"I've got a terrible cold," said Rip pulling out his handkerchief again and blowing his nose with a honk.

"We should be going," Willie pointed out.

"Well now," said Chauncey, as they stood up, "about this here place. This here's my home, but I'm too smart a homeowner not to know you ain't improving it. I'll make a deal with you. You don't tell no one else about me up up here, and I won't tell no one about you, and we all four use it together."

They agreed immediately, walked down the steps and up the street, still sniffling, feeling saddened, but at the same time happy about having a new friend. They said goodbye quickly and streaked for their houses, bracing themselves for the inevitable confrontation with angry parents.

Later, in bed, Willie's ulcer exploded in his stomach like a land mine. Tossing fitfully through the night, Willie wondered why it was so difficult for anyone not born and bred and fed and coddled in Squirrel Hill to have a happy life. Would Middlebaum be in danger of dying if he lived in Squirrel Hill? Willie would have staked his life on the notion that those people born good-looking and rich were permanently immune from such things. You are either born in a hole or on a mountain, Willie concluded. If it's to be in the hole, then no matter how hard you try to get out, scrambling, fighting and working, you will ultimately get buried. He saw it all in the dream he had: Chauncey and Rip and Middlebaum and Willie getting buried; millions of good-looking well-dressed people with madras shirts, pants with buckles on the back and diamond rings on pinky fingers, standing atop Squirrel Hill mountain, shoveling in the dirt.

Chapter XI
Crime and Punishment

"What happened?" Willie, Rip, and Middlebaum asked one another when they met the following afternoon.

"I'm not allowed out," said Middlebaum. "My dad said I used up all my staying out time for two weeks."

"You didn't tell about Chauncey, did you?"

"Never," said Middlebaum. "If anybody ever finds out about Chauncey, it won't be from me. I don't know any Chauncey, never heard of a Chauncey. Chauncey who? Even if the Nazis strapped me in an electric chair, tickled my feet, and dripped water on my head, I wouldn't squeal on Chauncey.

"But my dad was really mad," Middlebaum continued. "He's not going to talk to me for a year. This morning he even gave me some chalk so we could write each other notes in emergencies."

Middlebaum's father was a tall, silent, expressionless almost featureless person who reminded Willie of an old shoelace. He was also a very gray man, the grayest Willie had ever seen, gray as a Confederate soldier, gray as the color of Middlebaum's layer upon layer of gray paint house. Willie could also make out some gray tinge taking over Middlebaum's face as the boy grew older.

"Your father never talked to you that much anyway," Willie said, shrugging.

"Twenty-four," said Middlebaum.

"What?"

"Twenty-four words my father said to me last week. But the week before he only said seventeen. Things were getting better."

"You were making progress," said Rip.

"Yeah, but the problem was, he wasn't saying too many different words. He used the same word eighteen of the twenty-four times."

"What word?" asked Willie.

"Shut up."

"What for?" said Willie. "What did I do?"

"I'm not telling you to shut up, I'm telling you that 'shut up' is the word my father always uses. Every time I say something, he says 'shut up.' "

"Doesn't your father like you?"

"Of course, he likes me. He loves me. It isn't that. You see, he owns a butcher shop."

"So?"

"So he's very nervous because he can't stand the sight of blood. He spends many nights after work in the bathroom, vomiting. He can't hold any food down. That's why he's so skinny."

"But you're skinny like your father, and you don't vomit all over the place."

"But I love meat. I love all food. I can't get enough of it. I eat ten meals a day, seven days a week, and lose two pounds a year."

"Why doesn't your father quit the business?"

"He can't, that's all he knows, cutting meat."

"He could learn something else."

"My mother says he doesn't have time to learn anything else because he's always too busy at the butcher shop cutting meat."

Willie had long ago been introduced to Mrs. Middlebaum when she started bringing Ronald to the Heinemann house to play. She was a dark, dry ragtag sort of lady who reminded Willie of a scarecrow. As time passed and the boys grew older, she sometimes came to visit without Ronald, and sometimes even came to visit without shoes, but whenever she came, she never failed to bring a jar of Jergen's Lotion along. And while she sat and gossiped and sipped coffee with Willie's mother, Mrs. Middlebaum would pour the lotion into her hands and rub coating upon coating into her elbows, knees, and cheeks.

Willie would often slip down into the basement, press his ear against the ventilation duct, and listen to their conversation.

"He's so stupid," he once heard Mrs. Middlebaum say. She spoke with such a heavy nasal twang that the words sounded as if they were coming directly out of her nostrils. "Ronald is so damn stupid, I just hate it. He's always sick. He's always causing trouble. At dinner, he sneezes into his soup and spills stringbeans onto the floor. He eats oatmeal with his fingers. Sometimes he hides under the table when I'm having breakfast."

"Why does he do that?"

"To touch my varicose veins. He says they're beautiful."

"Oh my," said Mrs. Heinemann.

"I tell you, I can't stand it. Everytime we plan a vacation, he goes into the hospital. Everyday, I buy another bottle of pills. Oh, I can't stand it. Everything has gone wrong in my life from the moment that kid was conceived."

Willie wondered why Mrs. Middlebaum didn't get rid of her son. What was the point of keeping a kid around who was going to die any second? What was the point of manufacturing such a kid in the first place? Wouldn't it have been easier in the long run if God had just made grown-ups? Then no one would have to suffer the torture of being a kid; everyone would be equal from the beginning.

"What bothers me most," Willie's father had fumed when Willie had come home after being with Chauncey that evening, "is that you didn't have the sense to call us and tell us you'd be late."

"If I had done that, you would have ordered me home."

"And you should have been home."

"That's why I didn't call."

"Your wise mouth is going to keep you in this house for a long time to come."

Willie shrugged. He didn't care. He was too tired and upset to care right then. It was 1 AM. Willie could not remember when his parents had stayed up this late or screamed this loud.

"After all we've done for you," said his father.

"And sacrificed," said his mother.

What have you done for me? What have you sacrificed?

"You didn't even have the courtesy to open the garage door for me," said Harry Heinemann.

Not this again, Willie shuddered. Harry opened up the garage door every morning to take the car out when he went to work. Willie had to close the garage door when he went to school and then open it again before his father came home. But the procedure never made much sense. If the door were open in the morning, the chances were comparatively favorable, barring a tornado or tidal wave, it would still be open at night.

"What's the purpose of closing it?" Willie once asked his father. Willie had learned since then that the less he asked his father, the less his father would have to answer; they got along much better that way.

"The weight," his father had said.

"The weight?"

"The weight of the door isn't good for the hinges."

"But," said Willie, proud of his ability to figure things out quickly, "the door weighs the same whether it's open or closed. And opening and closing the door is not so good for the hinges either."

"When the door is closed," his father grumbled, "it's not hanging on the hinges."

"I don't understand."

"You don't understand what?"

"What's it hanging on to, if it isn't hanging on the hinges?"

"It's not hanging on anything; it's leaning on the floor." Harry glared at his son for a moment, then turned away. "Now don't ask questions."

"If I don't ask questions, then I won't learn answers," he told his father. "You want me to learn things, don't you? You want me to be good in school."

"That's enough," his father warned. "Now get out of here . . ."

"Besides," Willie pressed on, "if the weight is bad for the hinges, then it's probably just as bad for the floor."

That was the last time Willie had questioned the wisdom of the garage door, but certainly not the first time he had gone to bed without supper for a whole week straight.

But facing his father at 1 AM, the night of their adventure with Chauncey, Willie realized that this time the punishment would be even worse.

"You're to come home directly after school and go directly to bed. You're not to have any supper."

"For how long?" Willie wanted to know.

"Until further notice."

"Until further notice?" Willie gulped.

"Until further notice?" Middlebaum yelped the following morning.

"How long is 'until further notice?' " asked Rip.

"As long as it takes for me to nag my mother enough to convince her to nag my father into terminating the sentence and putting me on parole."

"Good thing you're not Chauncey."

"If I were Chauncey, I'd probably end up in bed without supper for the rest of my life."

"Being in bed without supper is better than being in jail," said Rip.

"How much better?" asked Willie.

"Not much," said Middlebaum.

"What happened to you?" Willie asked Rip. "What's your punishment?"

"Nothing. My parents don't believe in punishment."

"That's because you live so close to Squirrel Hill," said Willie.

"Where I live has nothing to do with it. My parents say that punishment damages a child's spirit. And misbehavior is an integral part of the juvenile creative process. It has nothing to do with where I live. My parents are just smarter than yours."

One day went by, two days, three days, with no progress being made on Kiner's dugout; three precious Middlebaum days wasted, swallowed by useless time. What would happen if Middlebaum died three days too soon? What would happen if three days before the ribbon-cutting ceremonies and the party they were planning with the beer and the girls, Middlebaum kicked off? Harry Heinemann would be responsible. Indirectly, Willie would be responsible by virtue of being Harry's son.

"They can't do this to us," said Willie to Middlebaum and Rip at school.

"Chauncey says that the strong choke the weak," reported Rip who visited Chauncey each day after school. "He says that the rich sit on the heads of the poor."

"Chauncey's right," said Middlebaum.

"Of course, he's right," said Rip.

"People are always taking advantage of us," said Willie.

"No one better ever sit on my head," said Middlebaum.

"Actually, there's no hurry." said Rip.

"To sit on my head ?"

"No, to finish the dugout."

What did Rip know? What did he care? Rip had all the time in the world, but Middlebaum was going downhill by the day, could be biting the dust any second. "That's what Chauncey could have said when they put him in jail, but it's the principal of the thing, don't you see?"

"You're right," said Rip.

"Find out what Chauncey thinks we should do," said Willie.

"Revenge," reported Rip the next morning. "Aside from whiskey, Chauncey says there ain't nothing sweeter, purer, and more heart-warming, than good old-fashioned, two-fisted revenge."

"Revenge," cried Middlebaum.

"Revenge," said Willie.

"Revenge," confirmed Rip.

Chapter XII
Revenge

"What exactly *is* revenge?" Middlebaum asked.

"Revenge is the process," Rip declared, cocking his finger and lifting his brow, "by which you get back somebody who has gotten you first."

Middlebaum and Willie nodded and went to their classes, but the three boys were strangely silent that day and all through the next. They worked hard in class, walked back and forth from school, and went directly to their bedrooms to sit in isolation through the night without complaint, ignoring their parents mercilessly.

Willie had never felt such awesome lust before. His brain was filled with movies of how he could get his enemies back. Enemies were suddenly everywhere, every face he saw, every footstep that fell outside his window, every person in every car that zoomed and vroomed up and down the street. Zeewee and Kenner were enemies for being mean to Middlebaum. Slippers and Sparks were enemies for being teachers. His parents were enemies for not living in Squirrel Hill. Middlebaum's parents were enemies for torturing and imprisoning a dying son. They were all targets of his wrath.

All the people Willie could remember who had ever embarrassed, ignored, or laughed at him appeared in the pictures that flashed in front of his eyes as he sat in the theatre of his room. All other concerns had vanished: Middlebaum's death, dugout work, ulcer pain, nothing was as important, as meaningful, as this all-consuming hunger for revenge. It was both a terrible and wonderful disease.

A very special day came up at Herbert Hoover Grade School not long after. The Squirrel Hill Chapter of the Women's Society of the Pittsburgh Historical Foundation was showing their dramatic film, "Three Rivers, George Washington and You"—the same film they had shown every year at Herbert Hoover Grade School for as long as Willie had been a student. As a treat, after the movie, the Society traditionally provided cherry Kool Aid punch and bakery-made, extra soft, extra large chocolate chip cookies, served in the gym.

Willie, Rip, and Middlebaum and most of the rest of the kids had seen the film so often they could almost play the parts of George Washington, William Pitt, and General Braddock from start to finish by heart. They knew it so well, they could even recite the lines of the Indian Chief whose braves were attacking Fort Pitt—even though the Chief spoke exclusively Mohawkese. Yet, two periods of classes were always cancelled the afternoon the film was scheduled, and the entire school would gather in the auditorium in the dark to giggle, poke each other, and throw spitballs.

Before joining Slippers's class in the auditorium, they went to the boys' bathroom and sat on toilet seats, smelling the piss and hanging their heads in sadness. As he sat there, Willie wished he could tell Middlebaum and Rip how much he missed being with them. He couldn't work up the courage, but sensed that his friends knew what he was thinking, and that they were thinking the same thing, too. For a while, they stared morosely at the sinks and urinals without speaking. A long time passed.

"I guess we gotta go," Rip said finally, "before Sparks finds us here."

They nodded and went out the door, their tennis shoes squeaking against the floor. But halfway down the hall, Middlebaum stopped and pointed at the doors to the auditorium. "Hey," he said, "they're closed."

"Which means that the lights are out," said Rip.

"We can't get in," said Willie.

"What are we going to do? We're in big trouble now."

Middlebaum paused, then raised his eyebrows and shook his head. "No, we're not. Each teacher has to make sure everyone in their class is present before the program can start. Anyone missing is reported to Sparks. That's the rule. I sneaked out one time and hid in the girls' locker room for 15 minutes before Sparks found me, and they were still waiting to start the program when she dragged me in. They must have made a mistake and counted us in, because they wouldn't have started the movie if they knew we weren't there."

As Middlebaum talked to his friends, the boy's eyes began to sparkle. His whole face beamed. The ping pong ball started going like crazy, while his bony body was bouncing up and down on the springs of his soles. "You remember Chauncey telling us how he discovered that the Beechwood Boulevard Bridge was his home? Remember? He said it just came to him, this voice in the back of his head he could hear as clearly as he could his own name, saying that the bridge was his home, that living there forever was exactly what he wanted to do. You remember that?"

"Yeah," said Willie. "So?"

"So," said Middlebaum, "that same voice is now talking to me."

Without another word, Middlebaum bounced down the hall towards Slippers's room. When Willie and Rip hesitated, Middlebaum stopped, turned, and faced them. "What's wrong. You guys chicken?"

"I don't know if we should do anything bad here in school," said Rip.

"But it's a perfect time. Nobody even knows we're missing. Did you forget our pledge of revenge? Don't you want to get back at those bastards?"

"Well, I don't know about getting back at them today. I wasn't really ready today," said Rip.

"Why not?"

"For one thing, it's Friday."

"So?"

"So that's the Sabbath."

"You're not religious," Middlebaum said, "and besides, Sabbath isn't until sundown."

"My parents are religious, and they say Sabbath is on Friday, whether the sun is up or down. This is the Lord's Day, they say. The Lord deserves His due."

"The Lord can have all the dew He wants, but we deserve revenge," said Middlebaum, turning and swaggering into Slippers's room. Willie followed. No one could call Willie the Heinemann a chicken, even if it were true. Rip dragged in a few seconds later.

Middlebaum went directly to his desk, pulled open a side drawer and took two small packets out of a large plastic bag he kept filled to the brim with medicines for emergencies. Then he headed over to the front of the room and picked up three newly sharpened pencils from Slippers's desk. He also took something out of her top drawer

—Willie couldn't make out what it was—and slipped it deftly into his bluejeans pocket. Then he strutted over to Willie and Rip.

As he watched, Willie immediately sensed that there was suddenly something different about Middlebaum. Here was a new man. No longer the bumbling awkwardness, the insecure steps in five different directions. For the first time since Willie had known him, Middlebaum actually seemed to know what he was doing.

"You ever hear of the Phantom of the Opera?" Middlebaum asked, his eyes shining.

"It was a movie," said Rip, "about a guy who did things—killed people—at the opera."

"What's that got to do with anything?" asked Willie.

"The Phantom of the Opera was the sneakiest bastard in the world," said Middlebaum. "He must have killed a hundred people, and no one ever caught him."

"Look Middlebaum, I'm not going to kill anybody," said Rip, "so forget it."

"We almost killed Chauncey just last week," said Willie. "A murder a month is enough."

Middlebaum turned, walked out the door and down the hall. He went past the boys' bathroom, down the steps, around the auditorium, down a second flight of steps and into the gym. Willie and Rip followed reluctantly; curiosity was killing them.

Wooden benches had been set up in the gym for the kids to sit on. There was also a long table with trays of cookies, napkins, tubes of paper cups and a tall aluminum urn, filled with red Kool Aid punch.

Middlebaum walked toward the far corner of the gym, disappeared into the locker room, then reappeared, holding in his hand a black and white P.F. Flyer tennis shoe. Calmly, he carried the shoe across the room and raised it high in the air by its dirty, tattered lace. Middlebaum paused and looked around. He smiled to his right and smiled to his left, dangled the shoe as high as his arm could reach, and then dropped it directly into the urn. The black and white high-top P.F. Flyer tennis shoe hit the red Kool Aid punch with a plunk.

Willie and Rip peered inside the urn, watching the shoe disappear down to the bottom. At any other time, they might have tried to stop their friend from doing further damage, but right now they were simply too shocked to move. All Willie could manage was a look at Rip, and all Rip could manage was a glance at Willie, their eyes momentarily meeting and silently agreeing that Middlebaum had quite simply gone mad.

Middlebaum pulled from his pocket the two items he had taken from his medicine collection. Willie peered over his friend's shoulder and read the lettering on the familiar blue and white cardboard containers: Ex-Lax Chocolate Laxative.

Middlebaum broke the Ex-Lax into tiny pieces, sweeping them into his hand and carrying them to the serving table. Pulling up a chair and situating himself, he began to press the pieces of Ex-Lax one by one into the bakery-made, extra large, extra soft chocolate chip cookies.

As he watched, Willie finally began to recognize the importance of this moment. Middlebaum was absolutely right. There was no better time to strike back. To get those bastards. To wreak revenge on people. To mutilate their enemies. All of a sudden, Willie was no longer afraid of the consequences of his actions; no longer afraid of getting caught or getting punished. All he could think of was his insatiable appetite for revenge.

Willie rushed across the room to join in on Middlebaum's madness.

By the time Willie and Middlebaum had finished "spiking" the cookies and started poking holes with the newly sharpened pencils into the bottom of every paper cup in sight, Rip, too, had become infected by this sweet mania for revenge and plunged in to help.

When the three finished, they stacked the cookies and straightened up all around, so that no one would know anything had been tampered with. And then Middlebaum added the crowning touch. Willie and Rip were ecstatic as they watched their friend in his grand finale. Whatever might happen to Ronald Middlebaum in the future, the boy would always have this moment of his greatest glory and highest achievement.

Middlebaum had in his hand a tube of red lipstick. This was what he had stolen from Slippers's desk drawer. He took the lipstick, lifted the urn, and wrote a secret message directly on the table under it, then replaced the urn.

"What are you doing?"

Middlebaum turned his back. He didn't want them to see. This was his little surprise. "You'll find out," he promised.

Now they were in the bathroom, sitting and waiting for the

assembly to conclude, listening to each other's excited breathing, knowing that if they even tried to talk, they would immediately start to laugh, and that once they started to laugh, they would never, not ever in a thousand years, be able to stop.

When they heard the scraping seats and rustling feet from the auditorium, they slipped out of the bathroom and fell in with the rest of the students.

Down in the gym, Willie and Rip and Middlebaum watched while Zeewee elbowed his way to the front of the food line, grabbed three cookies and ladled himself a paper cup of punch. But by the time Zeewee walked across the gym and sat down beside Kenner, his cup was empty. "Who stole my punch?"

Wait a minute," said Kenner, staring down at his empty cup. "My punch is missing, too. What's going on?"

Finally, it was Middlebaum's turn. Most of the gym floor was now puddled with punch, but in all the confusion, no one seemed to realize it. Middlebaum filled his cup and watched the punch hose through the bottom in a red stream. "My cup is pissing," he said.

"So is mine," Willie said.

"There's a hole in the bottom of my cup," Rip complained.

Now it all seemed to jell. Somebody had played a trick on the entire class. It was sabotage.

Everyone was angry, Zeewee and Kenner included, but no one was angrier then Ronald Middlebaum. "Who did this? I'll punch out his guts; I'll burn out his gizzards. I'll beat up his feet," he raved.

Bernadine Levine discovered an additional supply of paper cups in the storage room and began serving up the punch personally, calming things down. Many of the kids gathered around her, embroiled in a contest to see how many cups-full they could drink, non-stop. But just as everything seemed to be going all right once again, Bernadine spotted the tennis shoe down at the bottom of the urn and lifted it out with the ladle.

"Hey look, it's a P.F. Flyer!" Willie yelled.

"Somebody was soaking their feet in the punch," Rip said.

"The Women's Society is trying to give us athlete's foot," said Willie.

"Or hoof and mouth disease," said Rip.

Middlebaum turned to Bernadine Levine. "Whose shoe is it?"

"How am I supposed to know?"

Middlebaum shrugged. "Maybe there's a name inside."

Bernadine gritted her stainless steel teeth with distaste and pulled back the tongue of the punch-soaked shoe to peer inside. "Yes," she said.

"Who?" asked Middlebaum.

"Zeewee."

Miss Slippers glared across the room at Zeewee, arching her eyebrows and cocking her head with Lana Turner-like indignation. "How could you?"

"Me? You mean me?" Zeewee looked up, poking his chest with his finger.

"You should be ashamed of yourself, young man."

"But I didn't do it, Miss Slippers."

"Is that your shoe?"

"It looks like it, but I don't know how it got in the punch. I didn't do it."

"I don't care who did it. You mop up the punch. Don't miss a drop."

Zeewee skulked into the cloakroom, got a mop, and went to work.

The Women's Society had supplied plenty of cookies, and Middlebaum, feeling sorry for Zeewee, brought over a couple of the "special" variety for him to munch on. "Eat," Middlebaum said, "it will make you feel better."

Although he accepted the cookies, Zeewee eyed Middlebaum suspiciously.

"That's what my mother always tells me to do when I'm feeling bad. Eat," said Middlebaum. "That's what she tells me to do when I'm feeling good, too, or when she wants me to shut up or get out of the house."

Willie, meanwhile, was serving Slippers a plate of cookies of the same "special" variety, and a fresh cup of punch. She thanked him, told him he was a good little boy, and patted him on top of the head.

"You better start to clean up," Slippers turned to Bernadine as she munched daintily. "The period is almost over."

Just then, Sparks appeared in the doorway, wrinkling her carrot-colored nose in confusion. "What's going on here?"

As soon as Slippers explained what had happened and who was responsible, Sparks stomped over to Zeewee. But at first she remained silent and watched while he mopped. As she watched, she smiled and winked and squeezed her ever-present white sponge ball, smiling and winking and wrinkling her nose in the most amiable manner, until Zeewee just couldn't help assuming that everything was all right, and that he had been forgiven, even though he was innocent.

Suddenly, Sparks's arm shot out and yanked Zeewee into the air. She had moved so fast, Zeewee didn't right away realize he was no longer standing on his own two feet.

All the kids, not to mention the delicate Miss Slippers, were shocked. Zeewee, the toughest kid in school, the Gorilla of Greenfield, was dangling like flypaper from Sparks's big boulder of an arm.

"So you're responsible for all this disgusting mess," Sparks said.

"But I'm not, Miss Sparks," Zeewee stammered.

"Then who is?"

"I don't know. Honest."

"I do," said Bernadine Levine.

Bernadine had emptied the urn and was about to wash it out when she discovered Middlebaum's message in lipstick letters which provided the name of the villain responsible for the day's destruction.

Sparks immediately dropped Zeewee. He hit the floor like a sack of potatoes. She turned to face Bernadine. "Who was it?" she demanded.

Bernadine looked down at the table, under the urn. "THE PHANTOM OF THE SABBATH," she read.

Later, after everything had calmed down considerably and all the kids had returned to class, Miss Slippers was discussing agriculture in Pennsylvania, pacing and weaving back and forth across the room with Willie and Rip and Middlebaum watching every sexy step.

"The wheat crop in Pennsylvania," she said, raising her forefinger to make a point. Just then she stopped, and her eyes grew as big and round as basketballs. In just a few seconds, Slippers took a deep breath, looked around the room, sort of moved her rear end cautiously from side-to-side, and began again.

"The wheat crop in Pennsylvania . . ." But then there was a sudden rumbling *splat* that echoed through the room. "My goodness," Slippers said.

Bernadine Levine, whose chair was directly opposite from where Slippers stood, sat up and wrinkled her nose. "What smells?"

"Don't look at me," said Willie.

There came another series of *splats* from Slippers's immediate vicinity. "My God," Slippers said loudly, surprised. "My dear," she said even louder. "My heavens," Slippers nearly yelled. She doubled over, holding her stomach. Her face was as red as her fingernails as she sprinted out of the room.

It was very embarrassing and disappointing for Willie to realize that a woman like Slippers could actually fart.

But he did not spend too much time dwelling on his disappointment because, just then Zeewee also doubled over and moaned. He too emitted a series of *splats* and *splotches* before jumping up and running out of the room.

Zeewee returned a few minutes after Slippers, both acknowledging each other's absence sheepishly and avoiding the curious stares from most of the rest of the class. But in a few minutes, Slippers had to leave the room again, and Zeewee soon followed. Soon after, other students also followed. Even Willie, Rip, and Middlebaum eventually followed and stood in line at the door to the boys' room, waiting their turn.

One by one, they all saw Middlebaum's final message, again in lipstick letters, on the mirror above the sink: "THE PHANTOM OF THE SABBATH STRIKES AGAIN."

After school was finally over for the day, Willie, Rip, and Middlebaum tried walking home calmly and quietly, like mature young men, but after just a couple of steps, they started to hop. Middlebaum's ping pong ball quivered so fast, Willie couldn't even see it. Willie got down on his hands and knees and crawled down the street, with Rip riding on his back. They got up and ran. They ran down Windsor Street, down Lilac Street, down Beechwood Boulevard, up the steps and under the bridge. They laughed. They pounded their fists against the wall, leaped over the dugout, bashing their heads into trees, laughing and screaming so hard they almost died.

Revenge, sweet revenge, was the ice cream of their miseries.

Chapter XIII

Out on Good Behavior

After school and on weekends, Willie, Rip, and Middlebaum worked very hard under the bridge while Chauncey sat and watched with whiskey-fogged eyes.

As soon as they finished digging the dugout, which was now 4' wide, 6' deep, and 8' long, they immediately began to plan for the dugout floor. On that day alone, Rip must have made twenty trips in and out of the dugout, measuring and re-measuring. "The dugout won't be big enough to fit four people comfortably. Somehow, I made a mistake," he confessed.

"Don't worry. If Kiner ever comes, I'll sit outside," Middlebaum said.

"No, I'll sit outside," said Rip. "It's my fault."

Willie didn't want to sit outside if Kiner came, so he changed the subject. "We have to decide how to put wood on the walls so it'll stick. The way I figure it, we could make mud, which will act like cement. We could stick the wood right on."

"That will never work," said Rip, "because it's too cool and shady under the bridge. The mud won't harden."

"Maybe we should install a furnace to warm up the place," said Middlebaum. "Or a sun lamp."

"Instead of wood walls, we could hang curtains," Willie said. "We could hammer spikes into the dirt all around the dugout and hang sheets or blankets down over the walls."

"My mother has some old curtains in the basement," said Rip. "I could take them. She'll never know."

"What color?"

"Blue."

"That's all right with me," said Middlebaum.

"Me too." Willie nodded, not so much in agreement as in acknowledgment, just so the talking would stop and the work continue. How many clubhouses had he planned in his life? At least two a year. How many tree houses, underground passageways, false walls, secret entrances had he started on weekends and in the summer without ever finishing? Four, maybe five a year. Wasted nails, wasted wood, wasted effort. Not now. Not this time. Finally, he had been smart enough to team up with people who knew how to get things done.

Why hadn't anybody ever told him before that having friends was a lot of fun? Why was it that everything important or helpful had to be learned on his own? There were so many things to find out that parents, neighbors, and relatives could tell you. If they wanted to, they could spread out before you everything you needed to know to have a happy life. But they wouldn't; they were always too busy, too tired, too upset to find the time. Except for Chauncey. He told them about revenge and how to get it. Chauncey had even taught them about love.

"Love," said Chauncey, early one evening as they huddled around the fire, "is when you like something or somebody more than you like yourself."

"Who do you love, Chauncey?" Middlebaum asked.

"I don't love shit."

"I don't love shit either," said Middlebaum. "I thought I loved Laurel Gibson, but I guess I don't, because I certainly don't like her nearly as much as I like myself."

"I'm inviting Bernadine Levine to the party, even though I don't love her," said Willie.

"We're having a party the night of our last day of school," Rip told Chauncey. "You're invited."

"Here?"

"Yes, we're bringing girls right down here to the dugout. Will you come?" said Rip.

"Boys," said Chauncey, smiling, shaking his head, showing his piano key teeth, "Chauncey is a partying man."

"Will you bring a date?"

"Never can tell. I got women here and there."

"We're going to blindfold our women," said Rip, "so they don't know exactly where this place is."

"We'll spin them around," Middlebaum said, "until they get

dizzy, so they can't keep track of the steps or memorize the turns from their homes to here. And then, when we get them down into the dugout, we'll give them a beer."

"And get them drunk," said Willie.

"And then we'll fuck them," Rip said.

"We'll fuck them to death."

"We'll fuck them like they've never been fucked before," said Middlebaum.

"And then . . ." said Willie.

"And then?" asked Chauncey.

"And then we'll grab their bazoongies. We'll squeeze them until they fall off."

*   *   *

From then on, they decided not to waste precious time meeting after school, but to rush home, change clothes, and get down to the bridge as soon as possible. More work could be accomplished that way. Theoretically, they had the whole summer to finish their project; *theoretically*, they didn't have to rush. But Willie knew, couldn't forget, that Middlebaum didn't really have the whole summer. They had to get things done before school let out. Besides, they all realized that it was more fun and exciting doing projects for a definite day and hour—a target time—when all must be complete.

It was like being the attorney for a man unjustly convicted of murder. He is innocent, you know he is innocent, and eventually he will be proven so, when the one and only witness to the crime returns from an African safari. But now your client is sitting in his dark, dingy, death row cell, with only minutes to live, and so far your efforts to turn up a new witness or find the missing one have been in vain. The guard brings in the prisoner's last meal, steak, potatoes and Jello mold. Back in the corner, a priest is grumbling in Latin and swaying back and forth like he has a stomachache.

Suddenly, the missing witness is found—the one who can finger the real killer and free your client. The brave young attorney looks at his watch. There are 27 minutes to execution time. And knowing that the Governor is the only one powerful enough to save his client, the young attorney jumps in his car and drives like a maniac at 150 miles per hour to the Governor's mansion, bursts into the Governor's private office, interrupts his dinner with his lovely daughter, who is actually in love with the young attorney, just as they are putting the hemp necklace over the innocent man's head and asking for any last words before he is hanged by the neck until dead.

Willie had seen Rock Hudson, James Stewart, and Raymond Burr go through this procedure again and again, and although he always wondered why they were never picked up for speeding and running red lights, or for that matter, why they didn't just call the Governor on the phone, it was very exciting to watch. And this was the kind of feeling Willie got setting deadlines, rushing around, frantically building and planning and pretending. If only the Governor or the President could commute Middlebaum's sentence. But no one, not anyone except God, could commute death.

He wished he could stop thinking about Middlebaum dying. He wished he didn't know anything about it, so it would just happen one night. Willie would wake up one morning, and his mother would say to him over the scrambled eggs, "Oh, incidentally, I meant to tell you, Ronald Middlebaum is dead." And then he could act genuinely surprised. "How tragic," he would say. Maybe he would even faint. But now, knowing that Ronald Middlebaum was going to die, that it was going to happen any day, how could he act surprised? How could he stop himself from blurting out, "Thank God it's over." Maybe he ought to practice the way to look and what to do when Middlebaum's death was officially announced. He could clutch his heart and fall to his knees . . . or he would have an ulcer attack, tumble down, writhing and wriggling on his parents' all-purpose, all-weather, all-color carpet.

* * *

He traveled down Beechwood Boulevard, Apache style, fifty paces running, fifty paces walking, watching the sidewalk carefully for enemy moccasin prints, avoiding imaginary twigs, cracks in the cement that, if stepped on, would alert the cavalry to his presence. Once, he thought he saw Chief Zeewee, the Army's top Indian scout, and he dove down behind some bushes in front of the Abuzzi

homestead, bellied his way across an open clearing, and took refuge in a swamp. He crawled through the underbrush and darted from tree to tree, diving for cover whenever an enemy appeared. But when he crept past Tanner's Indian Agent Shop, he was spotted by a patrol of blue coats, and he had to make a run for it, swerving back and forth along the trail so they couldn't get a bead on him with their repeater rifles, hearing the bullets zinging and zonging all around. He lost them in the Badlands where the terrain was rocky. When he finally reached the hideout, Middlebaum was already waiting, and Willie was puffing like a truck.

"Where've you been?"

"I saw Zeewee, and I thought I'd better make a run for it. I went through the back yards and lost him in the Badlands."

"Rip went to do some beer brewing. He said we should get to work out here."

Willie sat around throwing rocks and drawing designs in the dirt with his foot till he was breathing normally again. Then they checked the floor of the dugout and found some yellow stains on the wood where Chauncey had probably spilled whiskey.

"I wonder where he goes in the afternoons," Middlebaum said.

"He's probably getting drunk."

"He can't get drunk all the time. He must have a job. Everybody's got to work."

"Nobody's got to work," Willie said.

They found some branches, broke them into pieces, and made a dozen crooked pegs, banging each of them into the upper lip of the dugout with the back of a shovel blade. Then they poked holes into the curtains with the steak knife Middlebaum had brought from home, and finally hung the curtains on the branches. The finished product looked pretty nice until the branches started to break, one after another. When Rip returned, Willie and Middlebaum were standing at the edge of the dugout, looking sadly down at the curtains, slumped in a heap on the floor inside.

"What happened?" Rip wanted to know.

"I don't know. The branches didn't work. Maybe we should have used metal rods. That's what curtains are supposed to hang from anyway," said Willie.

"Well, if you ask me, I think the branches you got weren't long enough," said Rip.

"What do you mean 'long enough?' "

"I mean that the branches need leverage to hold. Geometric principles, you know?"

"No, I don't know," said Middlebaum.

Though Willie was sure it didn't make sense to Middlebaum, what Rip said did make sense to him, although he hated to admit it. "Fuck," he said loudly. He was beginning to resent the fact that Rip knew so much about scientific stuff without knowing or wanting to know anything at all about Middlebaum.

* * *

Their hand-constructed wooden platform made the ideal floor and fit almost perfectly when they lowered it inside.

This was it. The boys scrunched down inside to see how it felt. And it felt fine. The girls would appreciate the comfort.

"Classy," said Middlebaum, leaning back, closing his eyes, smiling.

When Chauncey arrived, the boys stood up and clapped. "Welcome home, Chauncey," Middlebaum said, "make yourself comfortable in our humble abode."

"This is the life," said Chauncey. "Now, not only do I got a roof, but I also got a floor. A man can't ask for any more than that."

It was a very tight fit, with Willie sitting on Chauncey's feet and Middlebaum draping his legs over Rip's knees, but nobody seemed to mind.

"What we need now is carpeting, wall-to-wall, like Rip has in his home. Now that's really classy," said Middlebaum. "And that's what we're going to have next. We should start to collect bottles again, and pretty soon we'll have enough for carpeting, furniture and a TV set."

"Hey," Willie said, bouncing to his feet, "why don't we go have a look at the beer?"

"Good idea," said Middlebaum.

"I don't know," said Rip.

"C'mon, we've never seen it."

"But it's still brewing; it isn't finished yet."

"I want to see it brewing."

"Me too," said Willie.

"OK, but it won't look like beer. That's what you've got to understand. Brewing beer doesn't look the same as already brewed and bottled beer."

Rip was carrying a food strainer in his back pocket which jiggled as he led them back into the weeds.

"How come you have the food strainer?"

"That's to skim off all excess foam."

The beer was in an old battered metal washtub, covered with a big piece of plywood. Rip pulled away the plywood and leaned it against a tree. Middlebaum and Willie peered inside, then bounded backward at least ten feet.

"OOOOOO," Middlebaum groaned.

"PHEWWWWWW," from Willie.

"That's terrible stuff," said Middlebaum.

"It looks like vomit," said Willie gagging.

"That's the way beer is supposed to be when it's brewing," Rip said. "You can't expect half-done beer to be like already-completed beer. Bread doesn't look like bread right away, either, you know. It looks like a tennis ball or a big hunk of gum. Then you bake it and it comes out bread."

"When're you going to bake this stuff?" Willie asked.

"When it looks like a tennis ball," Middlebaum answered.

Willie and Middlebaum tiptoed up to the edge of the washtub once more and peered back down inside.

"I think somebody shit in the beer," Middlebaum said.

"I think the beer is farting at us."

"I see a fly in there. No, I see three, four, seven flies."

"And there's a dead bee," Willie pointed, "and a dead spider, and another bee, and a caterpillar. And there's a dead moth."

"No wonder they're dead, they probably drank the stuff."

Rip slammed the plywood back down on the washtub and sat on it. "You guys can laugh all you want, but I'm telling you, this is really going to be good beer. It's just that it's still brewing. You can't expect it to look good now, but you just wait until the party."

Middlebaum and Willie were laughing, punching each other on the shoulder and rolling around on the ground, pretending that they were dying from the smell, yelling about how they would have to wear nose plugs and blindfolds when they drank. And at the party, Bernadine, Laurel, and Shirley would want to know why they were serving Milk of Magnesia and calling it beer.

Chauncey, who had been standing back and watching the boys perform, lifted up the plywood and looked inside. He stared down into that terrible tub for a long time, sniffing; he even had the guts to stick his finger into the brew and taste a drop. Then he looked up, closed the lid, and turned around smacking his lips. "You ain't goin' to believe it, boys, but as sure as I'm standing here, that goin' to be some mighty fine stuff."

"See?" said Rip.

"That? Fine stuff?"

"It ain't beer yet, I'll grant you. Right now it in 'the delicate stage.' But if it keeps brewing as it is right now, it goin' to be a real zinger."

"A zinger," said Rip, "I told you."

"Holy cow," said Willie, "we're really doing it. Boy-oh-boy, we're really doing something from start to finish."

Middlebaum put his fist up to his mouth. "Ladies and gentlemen, this is your favorite announcer, Ronald—The Wonderful—Middlebaum, and I'm speaking to you on location under the Beechwood Boulevard Bridge, right at the spot where they manufacture the famous Zinger Beer. Today my special guest is the brewmaster of the Zinger Brewing Company, Rip Van Wrinkle. Mr. Wrinkle, can you tell the viewing audience your secret of manufacturing what is known far and wide as 'the perfume of bottled beers?' "

Rip stepped up to the microphone, smiling and waving at the TV audience. "Bazoongie power," he said.

"Thank you very much Mr. Van Wrinkle. And now ladies and gentlemen of the jury, this is Ronald—The Wonderful—Middlebaum signing off for the Zinger Brewing Company of Kiner, Pennsylvania with one final message. Don't forget our slogan . . . 'There ain't one queer . . . who drinks Zinger Beer.' "

Chapter XIV
Beginning of the End

Willie and Middlebaum walked slowly up Beechwood Boulevard
on their way home to dinner. They had just finished a hard afternoon working on the dugout, and Middlebaum was chattering.
Willie, however, had lapsed into a morose silence.

"And you know what? You know what's the greatest thing about
what we're doing?"

Willie gazed up the street.

"It's endless," he heard Middlebaum say. "The dugout is almost
done for now, but there's always more to do later. Tomorrow we'll
hang the curtains back up, but someday we'll put plaster on the
walls. And, when the plaster dries, we'll paint. By that time, maybe
we'll want to make a lamp or table. Maybe the paint will chip and
the plaster will crack and we'll have to patch and paint again. There
will always be something to do."

Willie felt sinkingly sad, felt the agony of a hundred murders
and a thousand sicknesses on his back and shoulders. How long
could he endure the weight of his responsibility to Middlebaum
and the pain that this knowledge brought him? How long could he
live with the torture of the unreliable shifting of his moods?

"By the way, I told my mother you'd go to the doctor's with me
this Saturday," said Middlebaum.

"What did you tell her that for?"

"'Cause I knew you'd do it."

"But I don't want to do it."

"It won't take long; just a check-up."

"Why don't you go by yourself?"

"'Cause I can't; I need company."

"For what?"

"I'm too scared to go alone. I told you that before."

"Well, I'm not going," Willie said."

"If you don't go with me, I'll probably never get there."

"That's not my business."

"Yes it is, Willie, you're my friend."

"I'm not going," Willie said, as Middlebaum turned, waved good-bye, and started bouncing up the street toward home.

"Yes you will," he said.

"No," Willie insisted, but right away Willie realized that his protests were meaningless, and that he would do almost anything Ronald Middlebaum wanted or needed because, right at that very moment, Willie heard it coming. He heard it from a long way off, CLOPPCLOPPCLOPP, THUD THUD, dull and sharp at the same time, like a lumberjack's chopping axe. CLOPPCLOPP-CLOPPCLOPP.

A hole opened in the sky, and God's helicopter clopped quickly through, streaking down from the heavens and hovering over Middlebaum's bouncing head. Willie peered up. He could see into the cockpit as God put on His Nazi combat helmet and pressed the blue pea jacket button that activated the V-2 death rocket cannon.

Moses and Abraham, wearing matching coats of many colors, scampered out of the barrel of the cannon. They picked up a sleek, silver shell, slid it down into the cannon, nodded to God, then disappeared back inside.

Now, clopping and clattering, the helicopter moved about 100 yards behind Middlebaum's bouncing back. Then God pressed Middlebaum's pea jacket button. Smoke filled the air as the rocket streaked through the sky. There was an explosion as it hit.

When the clouds cleared, Willie could see that the V-2 death rocket had missed Middlebaum by inches, but a huge crater now loomed directly in front of Middlebaum's path. If Middlebaum wasn't careful, he'd plunge a million feet down inside. "Watch out, Middlebaum," Willie yelled.

But Middlebaum wasn't afraid. When he reached the crater, he simply walked down one side, down so far he must have hit the bottom of China, then up the other side, back onto solid sidewalk, ambling steadily homeward, as if nothing had happened.

Willie was surprised, but relieved. "Ha!" he radioed up to God. "Over."

God shook His head, tipped His helmet and shrugged. The

helicopter immediately disappeared.

But Willie's victory didn't make him feel any better. He arrived home so tired and depressed that his knees bent under the weight of his troubles.

"Well," said Sarah, "you're home early. Your father won't be here for an hour. What's wrong? You look tired."

"I'm tired."

"You're probably not getting enough sleep."

"I'm not sleeping enough."

"Or is it your ulcer?"

"Might be my ulcer." He was leaning against the wall at the top of the stairs, wanting very much to escape into his bedroom.

"Well," she continued, "it's unusually hot this spring, and you probably have a lot of tests in school which are tiring you out."

"It's hot in school," he mumbled, "and I'm taking a lot of tests which are tiring me out."

Finally, when the phone rang, and she ran to answer it, he was released.

He shut his door tightly and toppled to the floor. For a long time, he lay on his back, cupped hands pillowing his head, concentrating on the pattern of shadows made on the wall by the sun streaming through the blinds. He watched the particles of dust floating in the air. He studied the maze that a spider had knit in the corner. He concentrated on everything he knew to be in that room—but saw nothing.

He felt as if he were about to cry. How many months had it been since he had cried? He was a man now, or almost a man—he was nearing his thirteenth birthday—and men were not supposed to cry. Still, he wanted so very much to let himself cry. There were times at school, sitting across the room from Middlebaum and watching him, when all of a sudden he felt the tears, droplets bigger than the moon, gushing, rushing, but he had held them back. People would notice, make fun, ask questions. And then there were other instances like right now, when he felt the urge to cry, without anyone around to hear, to see, or to ask what was the matter. But it seemed to be impossible. Now I can cry, now when I'm all alone, God, please let me cry. He could not.

The next thing he knew, his father was rumbling across the old wooden porch, and climbing the stairs slowly, each step an effort, each stair a mountain. Willie ate dinner and watched TV. He put on his pajamas and robe and walked outside. From the porch, he counted Fords and Chevrolets as they hummed by. The sky was yellow. The sky was gray. The sky was black. Stars twinkled. Lights pierced the curtain of night. When Willie crawled into bed much later, he still could not cry.

*   *   *

Laurel Gibson was the first to remember. One morning, weeks ago, she had printed a neat "74" in the upper right-hand corner of Miss Slippers's blackboard, and every morning before Bible reading, she would reduce the number by one. First, there were 74 days until school was dismissed. Then there were 70, then 60, then 47, and 25, down the line.

Each morning the kids gathered around the blackboard and waited for Laurel to make the new number official. When she walked in, she would take off her jacket and hang it on a hook, spread books out on her desk and sharpen pencils. And when she finally strolled to the blackboard, picked up the eraser, wiped out the old number, and then neatly printed the new figure, a digit lower, the whole class cheered.

To Willie and to Middlebaum, school was not a privilege, not a factory of learning, not a place to prepare for the future, but just a terrible part of a never-ending, never-improving routine. School was a huge old bus roaring down a superhighway, a bus with gigantic windows, with nothing outside those windows to see, except when Miss Slippers pointed it out to them, except when she hollered and screamed and nagged until they looked.

Willie and Middlebaum would board the bus in the morning, find their seats, listen to the Bible, recite the Lord's Prayer, pledge allegiance to the flag of the United States of America, and answer "here" to their names when called. Then the bus started up with a clunk, and they'd begin to move down this strange highway, with Miss Slippers's melodious voice singing out the sights along the way. Alabama and Uganda, Leningrad and Monticello. Russians with fur hats and beet-red Communist faces. Africans taller then basketball players; pygmies shorter than Snow White's dwarfs. Here comes Gettysburg, Pennsylvania where Union soldiers wearing blue are fighting Confederate soldiers wearing gray, who are fighting British soldiers wearing red coats, who are fighting Roman legions wearing iron underwear and leather vests. Further on down the road is Leonardo da Vinci painting billboards advertising the Catholic church; Benjamin Franklin stands in the rain flying a kite with a picture of Nathan Hale on it (Nathan Hale, Middlebaum observed, looked just like Tab Hunter). Suddenly, the rain started to come down in thick streams shot from the 19th century hoses of the Chicago Fire Department. The Hoover Dam crumbled and the bus floated like a cork in the storming, raging sea. Inside the bus appeared a bunch of foreigners. They said they were looking for Noah.

The water disappeared and Hitler marched into Poland. Japan bombed Pearl Harbor. How much is six million? What's a Holocaust? A man dressed like a mailman, smoking a corn-on-the-cob pipe and wearing a gold braided usher's cap, appeared out of nowhere to say: "I shall return, I shall return." He climbed into a canoe, and two Apache Indians wearing "Cochise for President" sweatshirts paddled him away. Willie's ass itched. Middlebaum was always hungry. Rip scribbled notes in his loose-leaf notebook. This is what happened, week after week, day after millions upon trillions of days in a row.

But now, for Willie and Middlebaum, who stood shoulder to shoulder watching Laurel Gibson on this very morning, there were only 12 more days to go. Willie had walked into school one morning and seen Laurel Gibson inscribe a white "74" on the black slate. He had looked down at his books, tied a shoelace, played the game where you tried to shoot your eraser with your forefinger from the bottom of the desk up to the empty inkwell on top with one shot. Then he had looked up again, and there was Laurel Gibson once more, carving out a "12" and circling it once. Where had all the days gone? The weeks? The months had disappeared. School passed so slowly. The clock in the hall seemed petrified in position. There was always more for Slippers to say. The lines of words in his book doubled and tripled and quadrupled when he'd have to read them. Each day was an eternity, hours glued with minutes, glued with seconds; endless units he could see and feel, from one to 60, and then from one to 60, and finally from one to 24. Yet, the weeks and months passed like tremors of a dream. First, there were 74 days until summer vacation. Then there were 12.

Can Middlebaum hold out for 12 more days? For one more hour? God's helicopter was now taking daily reconnaissance flights over Middlebaum's head.

Chapter XV
Bleep Blomp

Willie dialed the phone, his fingers trembling. "Hello, is this the Levine residence?"

"Yes, it is."

"I'd like to speak to Bernadine Levine."

"Just a minute please . . ."

"Hello."

"Hello, is this Bernadine Levine?"

"Yes, it is."

"Miss Levine, my name is William Heinemann, and I was wondering . . ."

"Willie, why are you being so formal? We know each other."

"Not officially."

"What?"

"We've never been properly introduced."

"You're so silly."

"How you doin'?"

"Oh, I'm fine, how are you?"

"Fair to middlin'. Fair to middlin'."

"Good."

"How've you been?"

"Oh, fine."

"Good."

"So what's new, Willie?"

"Oh, nothing much. What's new with you?"

"Oh, nothing much, everything's the same."

"Yes, I guess it is."

"Well."

"Hmmmm . . ."

"Well."

"Ummm . . ."

"Well, I guess I better get off the phone now, Bernadine."

"Oh?"

"Well, I guess I'll be seeing you."

"OK, take care of yourself."

"Well, I'll be seeing you."

"Willie?"

"Yeah?"

"Why did you call?"

"I was just wondering something, but I can ask you later."

"All right."

"Well, I'll see you."

"Is it about the graduation party, Willie?"

"How did you know about that?"

"Rip already asked Shirley. He told Shirley that Ronald was going to ask Laurel."

"Is she going to go?"

"Only if Ronald asks her."

"Are you going to go?"

"If somebody asked me, I would."

"Want to go with me?"

"Oh, I don't know."

"All right, I'll be seeing you."

"No wait. I can go. I'd like to go."

"OK."

"Is it formal or semi-formal?"

"It's formal, but don't get dressed up. Don't wear anything fancy for God's sake."

"Is it in your clubhouse?"

"Sort of. Is that what Shirley said Rip said?"

"Yes."

"It's just a graduation party because we're getting out of school for the summer, and because we're going into junior high, and maybe we'll never see each other again."

"Oh, c'mon, Willie, we'll see each other every day in junior high."

"You never can tell."

"I think I'll tell my mother we're going to the movies. That's what Shirley told her mother. My mother would never let me go to a party in a secret clubhouse."

"Why not?"
"You know, Willie."
"I guess."
"Well, Willie, it was nice talking to you."
"Yeah, I'll be seeing you."
"Take care."
"You, too."
"Sure will."
"Sure was nice talking to you."
"Nice talking to you."
"Well, goodbye."
"Goodbye."
"Bye."
"Bye."
Willie hung up the phone, drenched in sweat.

* * *

They walked under the Mercy Hospital sign, through the doors and down the corridor, past people rolling in chairs, goose-stepping on crutches, and rushing figures, blurred in white.

The elevator stopped, and they got on and moved to the rear. It was the biggest elevator Willie had ever seen, and he immediately calculated how many sports cars, dead people or combinations of both could fit inside. Willie and Middlebaum got off on the fifth floor, walked down to the third floor, and took the elevator back up to fourteen, walking the corridors on each floor, gawking at sick people anytime they found a door ajar. Willie saw a priest in one room. Middlebaum saw a rabbi in another room. Both were bent over beds, mumbling and whining inaudibly in foreign languages.

They took a good long tour up and down the hospital highway, then headed down to twelve where they caught the elevator to two, and walked up to three where Dr. Penmore's office was.

An auditorium of patients was waiting, filling two rows of straight-backed wooden chairs, women holding babies, men leaning against walls, hands in pockets, smoking and sneezing. The nurse at the desk smiled clinically. Her teeth matched her hat. "You're late, Ronald. I was just about ready to call your mother. Those are our new orders. Anytime you don't show up, we're supposed to call right away."

"I'm sorry," Middlebaum motioned to Willie, "but I had to meet my friend who was visiting somebody here in the hospital."

"Oh?" The nurse looked clinically concerned.

"It's OK," Middlebaum said. "It's only his grandmother."

"She comes from Las Vegas," said Willie.

"She has a broken back from dealing cards," said Middlebaum.

"But she married a man named Abuzzi," said Willie. "He owns a grocery store and lives in Pittsburgh, and she comes back to visit him every time she has to go to the hospital. Mr. Abuzzi is an immigrant from Algeria. He can't speak English."

The phone rang, and the nurse turned away.

"You have to wait for all these people?" Willie whispered.

"No, they usually take me right away. I told you, I'm special."

"How long will it be until you're finished here?"

"I don't know. Sometimes I sit in one of the inside waiting rooms for a long time before the doctor actually gets to me. He has about a thousand inside rooms."

"I wonder what's the difference between waiting in an inside waiting room and waiting in an outside waiting room?"

Middlebaum shrugged. "Search me."

After Middlebaum was called from the outside to the inside, Willie looked around. Back in the opposite corner sat a nun with what seemed like two popsicle sticks growing out of her nose. Her head was tilted forward, and she was reading a magazine. In her habit, she looked like a penguin with tusks.

Lots of people were sneezing and blowing their noses. Fearing infection, Willie tried not breathing, but couldn't hold out. He figured that the safest course of action would be to breathe in the direction of the smiling nurse, however, for she was no doubt immune to all fatal diseases. Otherwise, how else could she remain alive day after day here on death and disease row?

Periodically, the doctor would walk back and forth from one door to another and Willie would see him. A stethoscope hung down his chest, and a cigarette with a long ash dangled from his lips. Wherever he went, a nurse followed behind him with an ashtray.

Soon, a lady with a hose coming out of her left ear walked from the inner waiting room back into the outer waiting room. The hose was connected to a big glass jar buckled to her waist in holster position. The jar had a lot of white stuff in it. She found a seat next to the nun with sticks.

The man sitting on the other side of her immediately started talking. This man had big earlobes, hanging like bubble gum, swaying each time he moved his head. He had a very deep voice, deeper than a buzzsaw, rasping and vibrating, reminding Willie of a phonograph record played at a speed much lower than it was made for.

"I believe in God," he leaned toward the nun, rasping and buzzing. "I believe in the Good Lord no matter what He's done to me." He laughed, and his laughing sounded like he was giving the nun the raspberries. While the man talked and the nun nodded, the lady with the hose coming out of her ear opened up the white jar and sniffed inside.

"I believe in the Bible. I believe in the Good Book. I believe in an eye-for-an-eye, a throat-for-a-throat. Bllllaaaahhhh." He gave the nun more raspberries.

Willie watched carefully. One thing was very strange. Every time the man talked, he had to press a red button in a black box that was sticking directly out of his throat. Willie stared at the man, wondering if this was some sort of loud speaker system with a hidden microphone.

"What's in the box?" the man rasped loudly, suddenly looking right at Willie. "So, young man, you're wondering what's inside, are you?"

Willie looked away, pretending he didn't hear, but everyone was watching him now.

"You, son! Don't be afraid," the man blared. "Bllllaaaah. Come over here, and let me show you my squawk box."

Frightened, Willie darted his eyes at the nurse at the desk.

"Go ahead, boy," she said, "Mr. Frost is very nice."

The last thing Willie wanted to do was go over and visit with Mr. Frost, or with the nun or, for that matter, with anybody else here, and he glanced over toward the inner waiting room door, hoping that Middlebaum would right at this moment pop out, ready to go.

"Bllllaaaaah, c'mon, son," the man said.

"Go ahead," the nurse urged, "it'll be all right."

Walking across the waiting room, Willie wished his trick knee would suddenly give in, that he would trip and break his leg, or that he would get woozy and faint, or contract some kind of disease that would make him topple over like a stuffed animal. But no such luck. There he stood in front of Mr. Frost. He braced himself.

"What's your name, boy?" the man blared.

Willie couldn't remember his name, but felt his lips moving and heard some words tumbling out.

"Well, Chauncey, it's nice to meet you," the man nodded. "Do you go to school?"

Willie thought about grabbing the box and running away with it down the hall, into the men's room, and flushing the black box and the red button down separate toilets.

"Do you go to school?" Mr. Frost repeated.

"Yes, I'm in sixth grade. Next year, I'll be in junior high."

The man thumbed the red button. "Are you sick, Chauncey? This is a good doctor we have here. He saved my life."

Willie nodded politely.

"He cut out my throat, cut the whole mother out, but he saved my life."

"He's a great man," said the lady with the hose in the ear. Meanwhile, the nun was reading silently through her parallel popsicle sticks.

"You want to make me talk?" Mr. Frost blared at Willie.

"No," Willie said.

"Sure you do. Just press my button, and I'll talk. C'mon, make the man talk, make the funny man talk," he blared, dropping his hands from the button and mouthing silent words for Willie with his lips.

To bring sound to those words, all Willie had to do was poke a trembling finger at the red button and bury it deep in the black box. Which he did.

"BLAAAHHH," the man said loudly. Willie jumped back. Behind him a couple of people were laughing, but he ignored them, stepped forward once again, and pressed the red button.

"BLAAAH BLOOOOOO BLEEEEE BLLOMPP," went Mr. Frost.

Willie poked again.

"BLAAH BLOMPP BLEEEEEP."

Willie tried a little tune.

"BLAAHHHH BLAH-BLAH-BLAH-BLAH. BLOMP-BLOMP."

Mr. Frost was laughing, as were many others in the room, but Willie did not join in. Willie thought it was very unfair for one man to be making robots out of other men, and though he suddenly hated Dr. Penmore for doing it, he hated Mr. Frost even more for allowing it to be done.

Without another word, Willie turned, walked out the door, went down the elevator and sat on the front steps of the building under the sun. After a while, waiting for Middlebaum to come out, Willie walked around to the back. There, on the ground, was a rock the size of his fist. He picked up the rock and held it in his hand, switching it from one hand to the other. He smelled the rock, listened to the rock, talked to the rock, waiting a while for it to talk back. It didn't. He looked around. He looked to his right and looked to his left, then he hurled the rock through a nearby window and fled like a cat down the street.

Chapter XVI
No More Pencils, No More Books

Then came the final morning of the wonderful day on which school was going to end. Willie lay in bed tingling.

He had been forced to bend books, follow highways of words across centuries of history, add apples to oranges to peaches to sponges to bananas, subtract thumbtacks and staples from notebooks and paper clips; it had been terrible, but now it was over, the school year gone.

He heard his father's shower water crackling against the plastic curtain. His mother thumped into the kitchen. Water wheezed from a spigot, the old teapot clattered on the stove, Al Noble blared happy music, dumb jokes, over the old white radio.

Willie knew he should be getting up and pulling on clothes, but he could not quite bring himself to begin. He wanted to savor every joyful moment of waiting, just as he did at Christmas and Chanukah when he saved the big and important-looking presents for last, eking out every extra second of suspense, untying the ribbon rather than breaking it, fiddling with the knot, stopping to scratch his head or tuck in his shirt, prolonging the anticipation, which was, in the end, usually more delicious than the gift.

Finally, rolling out from under the covers and onto the floor, he pulled on socks, bluejeans, high-top tennis shoes, lacing them quickly, skipping every other hole. Then he went out and down the hall.

Harry Heinemann was not in the bathroom now, but he had left in his wake a thick, hot-water haze that smothered Willie as he stepped inside and secured the door. White fog hung everywhere, painting the mirror, making the toilet seat too wet to sit on. Willie snapped up a Kleenex and wiped a hole in the mirror, once, twice, five full times so that he could see himself clearly without looking like there was fog on his cheeks. He threw the Kleenex into the toilet, splashed cold water onto his face, his hands, his wrists, then rubbed himself dry with terrycloth. He brushed his teeth with Colgate, swallowed, spit white foam, raced a comb through brown hair, and was done. Shirt, pen, wallet, invisible make-believe walkie-talkie, and then finally into the kitchen for milk and ulcer pills, and if he was lucky, nothing else.

As usual, his father and mother were staring around each other as Willie entered. "I really don't want any breakfast today," Willie whined, placing a hand lightly on his belly.

"What's the matter?" Sarah yelped. His mother grabbed at sicknesses as did his father at money. "Don't you feel well?"

"No, I feel OK, it's just that I'm not hungry. I'll just have my pills and milk and head to school."

"If you're not feeling well, your father can drive you."

Willie jumped. "I'm feeling fine. Fact is, I think I'll have two eggs and a couple pieces of toast. I'm starved."

"Sure," his father looked up from his food, "all of a sudden he's hungry, because maybe he might have to sit in the same car with me."

"Now Harry, don't start."

"Who's starting? I'm not starting. I'm just . . ."

"I just forgot I was hungry for a minute, but actually I'm really starved."

Harry eyed his son suspiciously. "All of a sudden."

Willie stifled the urge to say he wanted ten eggs and a whole loaf of bread. He tried to look innocent.

"He could be dying with a knife in his chest, and if I were driving the ambulance, if I were the only driver in the whole goddam city, he wouldn't go."

"Harry, how *can* you say that?"

Harry, how can *you say that?*

"You shouldn't even joke about these things," Sarah said.

"Who's joking? It's no joke. It's true."

"No it isn't."

Wanna bet?

"You're being silly," said Sarah.

"I'm always being silly. Your precious son is never silly . . ."

Willie was always his mother's son when he did something wrong, and his father's son those few times he managed something right.

"... Not your son, *he's* never silly, only the big, dumb, stupid father who works his heinie off to pay the bills is silly."

Good old Heinie Heinemann, Willie thought.

"You're right," his mother sang in soprano as Willie tasted his eggs.

"Sure, I'm always right, whenever you want me to shut up I'm right. But I'm not right. I'm wrong," he shook his head, "that's what you really think."

"You're right, Harry."

"I'm not hungry," his father said, pushing away the plate.

"So don't eat. I couldn't care less if you never eat."

"All right, I'll eat." Harry pulled back the plate and shoveled silently.

And here, ladies and gentlemen, Willie announced to himself, is a typical breakfast scene at the Heinemann's, a family who loves and cherishes each other. Tune in next week when we feature the sequel program, "The Heinemann's at Dinner," a truly moving account of the loved ones gathering together once more in never ending devotion. This program stars Rock Hudson as Willie, Jack Benny as Sarah and Kate Smith as Harry. And now, a word from our sponsor . . .

"Besides," said Harry, "this is the last day of school, and if I remember correctly, they start a half hour later on the last day."

"Well," said Sarah, "maybe it's different this year."

"He's right," Willie admitted.

"Then why go so early?"

"I don't know."

"He never knows anything we want to know," his father complained some more.

"It's just that I wanted to get outside. It's hot in here. The fresh air and sunshine will be good for me."

"He is rather pale this year," Sarah said, lovingly stroking his cheek. "Usually, by this time, he's got a little tan."

Willie did not say that that was because he spent all of his time under a bridge or locked inside a basement.

"All right, let him go. I never win an argument in this house."

Before they looked around or had time to change their minds, Willie vanished. They heard him yell goodbye from way up the street.

Willie was a trooper that morning, and he counted cadence as he trudged, head bent, to school. ". . . To your left, your left, your left, right, left . . ."

His feet bounced high as he slammed his heels into the cement. With each step, stiffened arms shot back and forth like a pendulum. ". . . To your left, your left, your left, right, left . . ."

He performed a couple of right and left obliques to dodge cracks in the sidewalk, marked time at intersections, and called out mighty "Column Rights," and "Column Lefts," as he turned up Lilac, then made a second turn up Windsor Street.

Middlebaum was waiting with Rip in front of the school, and the three paced around and around the asphalt school yard, ignoring first bell, second bell, third bell, warning bell, final bell. Then they went into school.

Slippers hadn't arrived yet; someone said that a teachers' meeting had gotten held over downstairs in the office. Bernadine, Laurel, and Shirley were talking quietly. The whole class seemed tense and nervous. As he sat down, Willie noticed a package on Slippers's desk wrapped neatly in white paper with red ribbon.

Soon, Laurel Gibson stood up and moved slowly toward the blackboard. The day before, Laurel had etched a big, white "1" on the board, surrounded the number with a wreath of stars, and bordered her design with a circle of exclamation points. She picked up the chalk, erased yesterday's design, and printed in its place a big, oval-shaped zero. She drew eyes in the zero and gave it a triangular nose, loops for ears and a smiling semi-circle of a mouth.

As Laurel created, Zeewee, Kenner and some of the other Greenfield Gang, went over to the sink to work on their own creation. They tore sheets of paper towels from the dispenser, rolled them into balls and wet them. When Laurel put the chalk back in the trough and started to return to her seat, Zeewee yelled, "Fire!" and a gigantic spitball splattered between her eyes.

Almost simultaneously, Bernadine Levine was splattered in the back of the neck while Shirley Millmaker got clobbered in the bazoongie. Middlebaum would have been the next and most obvious

142

target had he not instinctively taken cover in the bomb shelter under his desk. Then Zeewee and his boys began to chant:

NO-MORE-PEN-CILS . . . NO-MORE-BOOKS
NO-MORE-TEACH-ERS-DIR-TY-LOOKS
NO-MORE-PEN-CILS . . . NO-MORE-BOOKS
NO-MORE-TEACH-ERS . . . NO-MORE-SCHNOOKS

They started to clap their hands and sashay around the room like song-and-dance men.

NO-MORE-LEARN-ING . . . NO-MORE-WORKS
SCHOOL-IS-ON-LY-FOR-THE-JERKS

The boys went around and around, parading through the cloakroom, under Slippers's desk, up and down the aisles. Their chanting and dancing was so infectious, that Willie, Rip, and Middlebaum, as well as some of the other kids, were actually on the verge of joining in, just as the somber, hulking figure of Miss Sparks appeared in the doorway.

Within twenty seconds, the whole room was rocked numb with silence. Zeewee, Kenner, and the Greenfield Gang returned immediately to their seats. Then Miss Slippers made her entrance.

The morning passed and passed and passed, and finally Miss Slippers stopped returning old papers, emptying drawers, stuffing the tall gray filing cabinets with supplies. She stopped marking numbers and letters in her notebook, filling out the report cards she would soon be sending home to their parents, and stood up to face Willie and the rest of the class.

"This is the last time we will be together, boys and girls," Slippers sang. "This is the last day that you can say with pride to friends and relatives that Herbert Hoover is your school."

Willie thought, as she talked, that this wasn't necessarily true, that someday he might return as principal, or gym teacher, or as a soldier to lead the forces that would defend this building from Chinese Communist aggressors. He thought, as he watched her lovely Jane Russell ass flatten against the edge of the desk, that someday he would return as a merchant sea captain to sweep her off her feet, or that maybe he would be sitting in one of those cafes in Paris where you could drink on the front porch, sipping wine, and she would be sitting alone at the next table, and he would recognize her by her ass, and pick up his bottle, and walk over and sit down, and their eyes would meet, and they would walk off into the sunset together.

Slippers glanced down at the box wrapped in white with red ribbon. "Is this for me?" she said in surprise, as if she hadn't noticed that the box had been on her desk all morning.

The class was silent. Willie couldn't remember any talk about buying Slippers a present, and he certainly hadn't been asked for a contribution.

"Should I open it now?"

Everybody looked around, but nobody said anything.

Slippers shrugged a Lana Turner shoulder, untangled the ribbon, stripped away the white paper. It was a shoebox. She hesitated. "A pair of slippers for Miss Slippers?" She chuckled at her own joke, then peeked inside.

A sharp noise came from deep within her stomach and lodged in her throat, like a frog's croak. Slippers's face went white. She slammed the box shut and fell backwards into her swivel chair.

"Get out," she mumbled, shaking her head and burying her beautiful face in her delicate hands. When no one moved, she jumped up. The color of her face rushed from white to crimson. "Get out, get out!" she screamed.

Everybody looked around the room at one another, but still no one moved. "GO HOME," Slippers screeched. "PLEASE. GET OUT. GO HOME . . ." She slumped back down in her chair and started crying, softly at first, but the sobs grew louder, painful, choking. Black and blue lines of make-up streamed with her tears down her cheeks.

The puzzled children gathered up their books and papers and filtered out of the room in groups of twos and threes, departing Herbert Hoover for the very last time.

"Well," Willie said, as he met his friends at the corner, and they started walking home. He couldn't think of anything better to say.

"Well, well," Rip said.

"Well, well, well," from Middlebaum.

"I guess that's it," said Willie.

"That's 'it' all right."

"There's no doubt about the fact that that's 'it.' "

"That's as 'it' a situation as I have ever seen."

"Thank goodness," muttered Middlebaum.

"Thank goodness is right," Willie echoed.

"It's about time," Rip said after a while.

"Tonight's the big night," Middlebaum added.

"We're gonna have a great time tonight," Willie said.

"You're not kidding."

They traveled slowly and quietly down the street, feeling strangely vulnerable being released so early from their jail, even though they had been officially paroled.

"What do you think was in the box?" Middlebaum said.

"Don't know," said Willie.

"It was a dead bird," said Rip, "a gray pigeon."

Willie and Middlebaum stopped and asked in unison: "How do you know? Who told you?"

"Nobody told me."

"Then how do you know?"

"I put it there."

"What did you do that for?"

"Slippers was a pretty nice teacher; she never did anything mean to us," said Middlebaum. "Besides, she's our future wife."

"I just can't understand why I did it," said Rip. "It was a perfectly illogical thing to do; I guess that's why."

"That's why what?"

"That's why I did it," said Rip. "I've been thinking about it the whole morning and asking myself the same question. And now I've got it figured. I finally know why."

"So why?"

" 'Cause there was absolutely no reason to do it."

"That doesn't make any sense," said Middlebaum.

"That's precisely the point. It doesn't make one millionth of a decimal point's worth of sense."

"I understand what you're saying," said Willie. "We're always supposed to do everything that makes sense, right? So it makes perfect sense to do something that doesn't make any sense at all for a change."

"Everybody deserves a change," Middlebaum agreed.

"I found that bird two weeks ago in the woods behind the bridge near where I'm brewing the beer. Everyday, when I'd go to stir up the beer and skim the foam off the top with my strainer, I'd see this dead bird. One day, I saw a cat rip off some of its feathers, so I chased the cat, got the feathers back and taped them back on the bird's wings with Scotch tape. Then I stole one of my mother's shoe boxes and put the bird inside, wrapped it up, and put it on Slippers's desk early this morning. I couldn't think of anything to do with it; giving it to Slippers was all that came to mind."

"Glad it didn't come to my mind," said Middlebaum.

"Maybe it's how I feel about the way I've been treated in school," said Rip.

"But everybody thinks you're a brain."

"That doesn't mean they think I'm a person."

Willie stared intently at Rip as they walked down the street. He suspected that Rip wasn't telling the truth—or, at least, wasn't telling all the truth. Something else was troubling him.

"I'm going home to rest," Middlebaum said. "We're going to be out pretty late tonight, and I want to be in good shape."

"Don't forget. We meet at the bridge after dinner."

As soon as Middlebaum ambled out of earshot, Willie looked Rip right in the eye. "Why did you really do that to Slippers?"

Rip glanced over at him, then turned away. "I already told you."

"I know what you told me."

"So?"

"So I don't believe you."

They paused at the corner of Beechwood and Lilac for the stoplight. When the light turned from red to green, neither boy moved. "Well," said Rip, "if you know so much, what's your explanation?"

"Maybe you were upset over something," Willie said.

Rip pulled off his horn-rimmed glasses and methodically wiped them with a blue and white checked handkerchief he had dug out of his front pocket. "Oh really?" He tried to sound smug and only mildly interested, but his fingertips had turned white and the hand holding his glasses trembled. "What could I be so upset about?"

Willie shrugged. "I don't know. Not exactly. Maybe the beer didn't turn out right."

"You won't have any complaints about the beer," Rip assured him immediately.

They were silent again. The stoplight turned red, green, then red, but both boys remained rooted.

"You know, don't you?" Willie finally asked.

"Know?" Rip whispered. "Know what?"

"About Middlebaum."

Rip pushed a clump of black hair from his forehead, shoved the blue and white checked handkerchief back into his pocket. He stared at Willie for a long time. Willie stared back at him, searching for some sign of recognition, even the slightest hint that it might be possible to share their sorrow. But when the stoplight changed from red to green once again, Rip turned, trotted across the street and down Beechwood. He never looked back.

Chapter XVII

At the Cafe La Kiner

Willie dressed in khaki pants and a short sleeve madras shirt with a button-down collar. He modeled it by sucking in his belly and staring sideways into the mirror. Sometime between Willie's house and Middlebaum's street, the moon emerged, watching over the steel mills down by the river like an owl on a limb. It was a warm evening, but God had activated the fan in the sky to medium speed, creating a breeze, cool and pleasant, on Willie's cheeks.

He was feeling more relaxed now than in many days; his body seemed lighter and his stomach fluttered gently, as if someone inside was stroking it with a feather. The thought that Middlebaum was due to die did not plague him. He was weary of it, resigned to it, and deep down in his gut where things really counted, he still did not wholly believe it, could not completely accept it. How could Middlebaum die? Impossible, ridiculous, there was no sense to it; he might decide to take a hundred year vacation to Istanbul, but he would be back to finish high school eventually.

"Middlebaum, hey Middlebaum!" Willie yelled from the side-walk on Derban Street.

"Hi." The screen door flew open and Buffalo Middlebaum galloped across the porch and down the steps, panting like a puppy and smiling, the ping pong ball banging and binging in his throat.

Christ, Willie shook his head in wonder. How could Middlebaum have so much energy to laugh and bounce, especially considering his condition?

"What's the matter?"

"Nothing, just nothing."

"Well, you're shaking your head at me. Why are you doing that? I don't like it when people shake their head at me for no good reason."

"I have a reason, I have a twitch."

"Fuck you do."

"I do," Willie insisted. "My twitch comes and goes on a semi-regular basis. It was there a second ago, but now it's gone. It has to do with my ulcer."

"Well, I just don't like people shaking their heads at me, twitch or not. Especially tonight. I don't want to be made fun of tonight. This is our big affair."

They were going to have a bachelor party to sample the beer with Chauncey before going to pick up the girls.

Willie had had his share of beer before, mostly from the mugs of relatives who came visiting on Saturday evenings to sit out on the porch until late at night, talking with his father and playing cards. On occasion, he would also secretly gulp a taste or two from unfinished quarts in the refrigerator when his parents were out. Then he would stagger around the house, bumping into bookcases and cabinets, falling down and crawling on the carpet, singing songs and slurring his words, pretending he was drunk as a skunk.

Rip came out of his house right away, and walking down the street, the three little boys acted very grown up pretending it was just one of the many evenings they spent out together drinking beer with sexy women at their private club. Rip was wearing khaki pants and a madras shirt like Willie, and both Willie and Rip had on penny loafers. Middlebaum wore a new pair of bluejeans and a light blue tee shirt. As always, high-topped tennis shoes hugged his ankles.

Chauncey was waiting when they arrived, sitting in the dugout, pointing down to a lantern in his lap. "Looky what I got," he said, "all loaded with kerosene and ready to go. Stole it personally from my brother's basement."

Middlebaum struck a match, and they turned the lantern on, watching the blue-tipped flame for a while. "Now the girls will really think this is a cafe," said Rip. "All cafes in Europe have lanterns on tables."

"But we don't have a table," said Willie.

"This is an Egyptian cocktail cafe," said Middlebaum. "In Egypt, everybody sits on floors."

"You boys are sly devils," said Chauncey, "getting girls to come here. When I was your age, no girl would come within a mile of me."

"You stick with us, and we'll teach you all we know," said Middlebaum.

"As soon as we find out something," said Willie.

"Right. After this night, we'll tell you everything," Rip said.

"Boys," said Chauncey, "the more you learn, the more you realize you don't know enough to teach. Only people who don't know nothin' have the guts to try to teach somebody else. That's why we got so many stupid people in this world. One dummy passes on everything he don't know to a hundred others."

Rip went back into the woods to get the first belts of beer while Chauncey, Willie, and Middlebaum sat around staring at the lantern impatiently.

"I shouldn't be allowing you all to drink this beer," he chuckled. "You boys are too young to drink beer." Chauncey had dressed up in a white shirt and tie, although the shirt was no longer very white and the pointed tip of the tie had been torn off. Chauncey's shoes sparkled with fresh black wax, however, and new cardboard insoles had been inserted to keep the dirt and dust off his feet. "But boys have to have fun. They got to start somewhere—and as long as you made this here beer yourselfs, I don't see nothin' wrong with drinking it. Where is this beer anyway?"

"Hey Rip," Middlebaum called, "where the hell's the booze?"

Willie hooked arms with Middlebaum, and as they waited for Rip, they did a little jig around the dugout while Chauncey clapped his dry old hands and yelled "Olé! Olé!"

In a while, Rip returned with four bottles of beer. "Somebody put the beer in bottles."

"That the way beer is supposed to be. In bottles," said Chauncey.

"Brown bottles," said Willie. "I remember the recipe."

"That's right. I had the bottles ready and everything, but I swear I didn't do it," said Rip.

"Those are Budweiser bottles," said Middlebaum, pointing at the labels.

"That's the other thing. I took all the labels off my bottles. I can't understand it. The beer in the tub is all gone, the whole thing is empty—cleaned out to the last drop, and instead, there's these Budweiser bottles, all capped like they just came from the factory."

"You did it," Willie jumped up and pointed at Rip. "I knew

150

something was wrong. The beer you made was no good, so you bought these instead."

"Where am I going to buy beer? My parents don't even let me buy Pepsi, let alone beer," said Rip.

"Maybe the beer was so good that somebody traded us," Middlebaum pointed out, "somebody who had a yearning for good old-fashioned home cooking instead of factory-made stuff. They probably came across it in the woods and decided to trade us."

"Maybe it was Chauncey," said Rip.

"Boys, you wasting your time. All my money invested in whiskey. You know that good as I do. Anyway, I seen this here thing happen before in the South."

The little black man was chuckling, shaking his head. "Down in the South they got stills all over the place, for wine, whiskey and beer."

"What's *stills*?" asked Middlebaum.

"*Stills*," Willie informed Middlebaum, "is where they make illegal booze."

"You boys go and ask me to a bachelor party. You want me to tell you stories and teach you what I know, then you don't serve refreshments." Chauncey smiled. "Quit talkin' and start pourin'."

"But this might not be our beer," Rip objected.

"It yours now."

"Pour up or shut up," said Middlebaum.

Rip shrugged, set four paper cups down on the ground, then popped the cap of a Budweiser bottle with the opener Chauncey had in his pocket. Beer foamed out. Four hands grabbed cups and four sets of shining eyes looked down at the liquid.

But no one started drinking right away; they all sat in silence, regarding their beer and listening to the birds chirp night-time songs and the breeze brush through the leaves.

Chauncey raised his cup. "Well, somebody surely got to say something, and you boys are taking too long to think. A toast," he announced, "to my friends who share my home."

Willie waited for Chauncey to give some sign it was time to drink.

"May you live a thousand years," Chauncey continued, "and may I never die!" Then he brought the cup to his lips, threw back his head like a cowboy in a saloon—and drank.

There was a second, perhaps it was only a millionth of a second, when Willie hesitated, when he thought maybe he should cry out for everyone to stop and for Chauncey to repeat the toast again, for it was then that Willie realized that this great once-in-a-lifetime evening was finally started, which meant it would now begin to end, which meant that Chauncey's toast had little meaning, since sooner or later they would all die, except that Middlebaum was going to die first, and with each toast and each swallow and each beer, his death would be that much closer. Willie glanced up. Off in the distance, he could make out the red, blue, and yellow lights of God's helicopter observing them. Willie sighed, closed his eyes—and gulped.

"This beer ain't half bad," said Chauncey.

"It's all bad," said Middlebaum, wrinkling his lips.

"Beer is supposed to taste bad, and this tastes as bad as any beer I've ever had," said Willie.

"So it must be good," said Middlebaum.

"You made this stuff all by yourself? That's amazing," said Chauncey.

"I think I made it."

"Oh, you done made it all right. I can tell from the taste, and I know from my experience in the South."

"What about the South?" asked Willie.

"How about another glass of this delicious beer?" Chauncey stuck his cup out at Rip, and Rip opened up another bottle and filled Chauncey's cup and the rest of the cups all around.

"Now, what was I saying?" asked Chauncey.

"About beer in the South, it being illegal."

"Beer ain't illegal in the South. It's beer and whiskey and wine that ain't made by big companies that's illegal."

"You mean our beer is illegal?"

"Unless you a big company."

"We're not even a little company."

"My parents sometimes have company on Saturday nights," said Middlebaum.

"The whole world," said Chauncey, leaning back in the dugout and spreading his legs around the lantern, "is made up of people who are either with companies or not with companies. If you with a company, then you automatically immune from the law. And the higher up you get in the company, and the bigger the company is, then the more immune you are."

"What if you're not with a company?"

"If you ain't with a company, then the law gets you. It's as easy as that."

"God isn't with a company, and He's the most powerful person on earth," Willie said.

"He the President of Religion, the biggest company in the world," Chauncey pointed out.

"I never knew that," said Middlebaum.

"You keep going to school, you won't know nothin'."

"Anybody want more beer?" asked Rip.

Everyone swigged what they had and held out their cups while Rip snapped and poured another.

"I thought beer was supposed to be cold," said Middlebaum.

"That's what we need next—a refrigerator."

"But we ain't got nothin' to plug it into."

"I can make a plug in my workshop in the basement at home," said Rip.

"Let's toast plugs," said Middlebaum, raising his cup, holding his nose and drinking down more beer.

"To plugs," said Chauncey, Willie and Rip, drinking and toasting simultaneously.

"Let's toast refrigerators."

"To refrigerators," everyone repeated happily and chugged.

"To tennis shoes," Middlebaum proclaimed, holding up his black and white foot. "To good old P.F. Flyers."

"To good old P.F. Flyers," Chauncey, Willie, and Rip confirmed.

"To ping pong balls," said Willie.

"What the hell for? None of us are wearing ping pong balls," said Middlebaum.

"That's what you think."

"Anybody got the right to toast whatever they want," Chauncey raised his cup. "To ping pong balls."

"To ping pong balls," Rip and Middlebaum toasted.

"To toilet paper," said Middlebaum.

"To chicken bones," said Rip.

Chauncey and Rip and Willie and Middlebaum drank and drank watching the sun kiss the sky a final goodnight.

"This tastes better when you drink it faster," said Middlebaum. "The faster you drink it, the better it is."

"The bubbles are what's bad in beer, so the faster they go down, the less you taste it," Willie told him.

"*Still*," said Middlebaum, "that's a dumb name for a beer factory. The beer's lying still in the *still*. That doesn't make any sense."

"That doesn't make any cents, either," said Rip.

"Huh?"

"Forget it. I meant money. Forget it."

"The beer's still lying still in the *still*," said Willie.

"Still, the beer's still in the *still* lying still," said Rip.

"What happens is that companies are the only people allowed to make beer, and they charge so much money for it, only rich folk can afford to drink it," said Chauncey.

"Why is that?"

" 'Cause the government don't want no poor people to get drunk, that's why. They get drunk, next thing you know, they start revolutions."

"You mean George Washington was a drunk?"

"What do you think? You ever heard of the Whiskey Revolution?"

"And Ben Franklin and Nathan Hale? They were drunks?"

"Boys, if our forefathers would have sobered up long enough to realize what they were doing, revolting against the King of England, they would have died from pure shock and surprise."

"Nathan Hale said 'I only regret I have but one life to give to my country,' " said Middlebaum.

"Then they hung him," said Willie.

" 'Cause he was drunk," said Chauncey.

" 'Cause he was brave," Middlebaum insisted.

"It the same thing," Chauncey replied.

Rip poured more beer. Then they opened bags of potato chips and pretzels, distributing the refreshments in paper plates decorated with red roses. Rip had bought four giant economy-sized jars of olives stuffed with pimientos, and they built four mountains of green olives with red nipples on paper plates.

Middlebaum established a rule that nobody could take an olive from the bottom because the whole mountain would collapse. He checked out his theory by pulling an olive directly from the bottom, and he was right. The olives rolled into the dugout and on top of Chauncey, about a thousand in all, Willie guessed.

"Chauncey has red and green warts," Middlebaum teased.

"I also got an empty cup," Chauncey replied.

"I don't see why we bought olives anyway," Willie said. "I hate olives."

"Olives are elegant," Rip told them. "They come from Greece."

"Why did you put an olive in my beer?" asked Middlebaum.

"Olives are the elegantest in cocktails."

"The poor folks in the South," said Chauncey, "make beer in illegal stills. Then the government send the U.S. Marine Corps up into the hills where the stills are hid to blow them up with bazookas. But, in truth, when the Marines get up there, they don't do that. Instead of bazookas, they got empty bottles hidden in their trucks and knapsacks, and they pour all the illegal beer they find into the bottles, which automatically legalizes it, which quadruplizes the price. Then they sell it on the black market."

"You mean only Negroes can buy it?" said Middlebaum.

"Well then, maybe the Marines put our beer in bottles and plan to come back later and pick them up," said Rip.

"You got any other explanation?" asked Chauncey.

Willie did have another explanation. He had a couple of explanations, neither of which agreed with Chauncey's story. But it didn't really make much difference where the beer came from—at least right now it didn't—as long as it got there, and they were drinking it down like grown ups, one by one. If Rip or Chauncey or both had bought or stolen the beer instead of making it, it wasn't important. Not now. What was important was having a good time on Middlebaum's last, or second to last, or third to last night out. Willie fingered a beer-soaked olive from his empty cup and tasted it. He picked up another olive and put it in between two potato chips. "Hey, an olive sandwich."

"You mean an hors d'oeuvre," said Rip.

After a few more belts of beer, Willie noticed that it was getting dark. He said it was time to pick up the girls. They said goodbye to Chauncey, walked through the weeds, down the steps and up the street, swaying, pretending that they were drunk, knowing they were not, but strangely unable to stop pretending.

As they walked, Middlebaum ran out ahead, offering his middle finger to passing cars. "Fuck you," he told those cars, "and one fuck for you, and here's another for you."

"Pardon me, madame," Willie said to Rip, "I'm selling fucks. They're two for a dollar and three for 35 cents."

"Whoopie!" Rip yelled. "I'll take four and a half."

"Gimme eight, gimme eight," Middlebaum said, streaking back and forth, crisscrossing through people's front yards, doing little tap dances on strangers' porches.

As he watched his friend jump and dance and scream and laugh, Willie realized that Middlebaum was just like radio or television, and that anytime He wanted to, God could flick a dial and turn the Ronald Middlebaum Show right off. Willie was well aware that God's helicopter was following them at a discreet distance.

"I like beer and beer likes me," said Middlebaum.

"Rip's beer is great," said Willie.

"There ain't no queer who drinks Zinger Beer," said Rip.

In front of the Abuzzi house, Willie and Middlebaum laughed at the sight of Rip, his pant legs rolled up, his ass swaying and slinking in impersonation of Mrs. Abuzzi when she walks up the street. Willie and Middlebaum clapped and cheered as Rip bowed. The three boys then sat down on the Abuzzi porch sharing one of Middlebaum's Lucky Strike cigarettes.

"I should have invited her," Willie said of Abuzzi.

"Think she would have come?"

"She coulda gotten rid of her husband easy. She could have snuck out by telling him she was going to play mah-jongg."

"Well, it's too late now."

"We could have fucked her for sure," said Willie. "We all three could have fucked her till she pissed."

"We'll get fucked tonight anyway," said Rip.

"Fucky-ducky-doo," said Willie.

"Ducky-fucky-cucky-coo," said Rip.

To save time, they separated to pick up their girls. They planned to meet back at the dugout in half an hour. Everything had so far worked out well: the beer, the olives, Chauncey, the dugout, all going right. When they were alone, they could do nothing, but together, Willie and Rip and Middlebaum were perfect.

Chapter XVIII
Woof! Woof!

"You're late, Willie," Bernadine opened the front door the moment he knocked.

"Are your parents home?"

"They went to the movies. But what kept you? Did you hurt your back?"

"What's wrong with my back?"

"You're standing crooked."

Willie tried to straighten himself up as his eyes swept the living room; it was pretty classy, with a blue couch, two matching gold lamps, a coffee table with a glass top, and a cottony-plush orange carpet. So this was how it was deep in the heart of Squirrel Hill? If you're going to marry, his mother always told him, find a rich girl from Squirrel Hill whose father loves her.

"Too bad your dad's not home," Willie said. "I wanted to shake his hand."

"Well, they waited, but you were so late, and they promised to meet Dr. Goldfield and his wife at the movies."

Willie was impressed. "Do your parents know a lot of doctors?"

"I don't know, Willie. What's the difference?"

"My mother says doctors are fine people. Is your father a doctor?"

"He has a plumbing supply business."

"Plumbing supply people are fine people, too."

Bernadine looked very beautiful tonight in blue tennis shoes, madras shorts, and a white blouse that clung to her bombshell body. "Does your father love you?"

"Of course he does."

"You're wonderful," he told her, turning sideways so she couldn't see how his dick was pickling up in his pants.

"Are you ready to go to the party? I can't wait to see what Laurel and Shirley are wearing."

"Do you have anything to drink?" he asked.

"I'll get you something from the kitchen."

Willie stopped and turned in surprise. He had never before noticed how sexy and melodious her voice was. "Say that again."

"I'll get you something from the kitchen," Bernadine repeated.

"Your voice is very beautiful," he said, "and you look so gorgeous . . ."

"Willie, why are you talking to me this way?" Rivers of red flowed into her cheeks. Red reflected into her stainless steel mouth, as if her braces were also blushing.

He paused and tried to look dramatic. "Because I've never known a woman like you before," he quoted Rock Hudson.

She covered her face with her hands and turned away. "Willie, you're embarrassing me."

"You just sit there," he crooned, "and I'll go into the kitchen and bring us a little something to snoogle up with."

He bowed with a flourish and backed out of the room and down the hallway colliding with a lamp.

"Willie? What happened?"

"Nothing."

"You all right?"

"Yes, love bug, I'm just fine."

"I asked you to stop talking that way."

Her words and the thought of her bombshell body beckoned to him so strongly that he almost decided to forget the booze and return to sweep her up with his iron-fibred arms. But then he changed his mind; that part would come later. He would take his time and be cool, savoring that sauce of suspense that enhanced the taste. He swayed down the hall and into the kitchen where he rubbed his penis back and forth against the sink until it hurt.

When the doorbell rang, Willie rushed down the hall. "I'll get it, baby." Now he was talking out of the side of his mouth like a tough guy. "Who is it?"

"Middlebaum."

"How do I know you're Middlebaum? What's the secret password?"

"Kiner."

"That ain't it."

"Al Capone."

"That ain't it either."

"Asbestos."

Willie opened the door cautiously, his hand poised above where his shoulder holster might have been, ready at the slightest hint of trouble to draw his .45 pearl-handled automatic revolver and shoot the intruders down dead. But there was Middlebaum, standing so close to Laurel Gibson their shoulders were actually touching.

"We thought we'd pick you up and walk with you down to the Kiner Cafe."

Willie curled up his lip and sneered in his best imitation of a big-time gangster. "Who's the dame?"

"This is Laurel. She's a hat-check girl at the speakeasy."

Laurel, taller and skinnier than Middlebaum, lowered her head and giggled.

"I'm just fixing some drinks," Willie told Middlebaum. "You come with me. Your dame here can keep my broad company."

Willie led Middlebaum into the kitchen. "Christ, this is it," he whispered. "This is really it. This is goddam IT."

"Fuck-a-duck," Middlebaum said. "This is really something. This is really something. You mean we're all alone here making drinks?"

"You better believe it."

"Where are her parents?"

"At the movies with Dr. Goldfield."

"Goose-a-moose, rape-an-ape, screw-a-Jew. Do you think we'll get fucked?"

"How can we miss?"

Willie found beer and Pepsi Cola in the refrigerator. "The best way to make girls drunk is to have them drink beer and Pepsi together. The Greenfield kids call this Spanish Fly. It's the same thing farmers feed their pigs when they want them to get pregnant."

"How do you know?"

Willie shrugged. "No reason. It's something I just know."

Sitting down at the table, watching Willie, Middlebaum propped his chin on his fist and started snickering. Each snicker sounded like a little sneeze. "Heh, heh, heh, Laurel loves me. She'd marry me in a second, if only I said the word."

"Bernadine loves me, too. She really loves me. She just about told me so," Willie said. "That's what we should do, Middlebaum, you and me and Bernadine and Laurel, get married, move in together, and open up a plumbing supply business."

"Why plumbing supply?"

"I know somebody who can teach us the ropes."

"Heh, heh, heh," Middlebaum snickered. "Laurel's dad owns a laundromat. We'd always have clean underwear."

Willie took four glasses from the cupboard and filled them half with beer. Then he poured Pepsi over the top of the beer, almost to the rim. Middlebaum pointed out that the girls liked drinks that were sweet, so Willie put in teaspoons of sugar. They mixed it all up and took a sip, giggling at the goodness.

Middlebaum's head turned over to one side, but Willie set it straight with his hands. "Deedle-deedle-dunk, Middlebaum is drunk."

"No, I'm not. I can hear like a queer and see like a flea."

"You're plastered."

"Here's the plan," Middlebaum said. "First, we sit around and have a couple of drinks, and then I take Laurel into the other room. You stay in the living room with Bernadine. After all, this is Bernadine's living room, and Bernadine is your broad. If this was Laurel's house, then I'd get the living room. OK? I won't take 'no' for an answer."

"I won't give 'no' for an answer."

"Do you think we should put some aspirins in the drinks?" asked Middlebaum.

"What for?"

"To make sure the girls don't get a headache from all the beer."

"I'll put anything in; it doesn't matter. The more the merrier."

"The merrier, the drunkier," said Middlebaum.

"The drunkier, the fuckier," Willie added.

Willie found some aspirins in the cupboard, dropped one into each glass, and stirred thoroughly. He hid the empty bottles in the vegetable compartment of the refrigerator. Then he stumbled down the hall and into the living room.

Middlebaum was the fastest worker in the West. Already he had moved Laurel to the other side of the room and switched on the radio. There was nice music playing, although Willie couldn't recognize the song, since it was the kind of music that had no words. "Hey Laurel, let's have a contest," he heard Middlebaum say. "Let's see who can drink these drinks down faster."

Bernadine was sitting on the couch with her legs crossed in a very sexy position. Willie was very much in love as he glided across the carpet toward her. His arms trembled at the mere thought of caressing her. "Here you are, my darling, a special drink for a special girl."

"Willie? What's wrong with you? You're acting so strange."

"I think you're wonderful," Willie said.

Bernadine darted her eyes sideways to see if Laurel had overheard. But Willie didn't care; he wanted Laurel to hear; he wanted everybody in the whole world to know how he felt about that sex bomb, Bernadine Levine.

"You're acting so crazy" she said. "What's this drink you're serving us?"

"Is it good, my love?" Willie whispered.

"It's OK."

"It's a love potion," he said.

"What's in it, Willie? You better not have used any of my father's beer."

"Love juice," he moaned hoarsely, puckering up his lips.

When Willie reached over and turned off the light, he really started to feel wonderful. Even though it was dark, he could see Bernadine Levine blushing. The whole room was blushing, in fact, exploding with the gold and red glitter of his pounding passion.

"Well, I'm going to show Laurel your kitchen, Bernadine," Middlebaum announced, jumping to his feet. But then he lost his balance and fell backwards into his chair. He tried again, but as soon as he got up, his knees buckled and he sank to the floor. Finally, with the help of the coffee table, he managed to stand. "I really like your kitchen. It's the best kitchen I've ever been in, and I've seen a good many of them in my time. Laurel likes kitchens, too. It's her favorite room in the house. Laurel and I have a lot in common." Middlebaum nudged Laurel with his elbow and snickered. Laurel giggled back as they stumbled out of the room. Laurel was probably already plastered from the Spanish Fly.

Surely Bernadine knew what was going to happen next. She had been waiting for years for this opportunity to form a union with Willie. She hadn't protested when the lights went out, not even when Middlebaum and Laurel evacuated to the kitchen. Willie moved closer, so close that their shoulders and thighs traded warmth.

"Willie, I want to talk with you," Bernadine said, moving away from him. "We think that you're both drunk; that's the way you're both acting, like you're drunk."

"Drunk with my love for you," he told her, amazing himself with the good lines he was coming up with. He moved close to her again, and dangled his arm around her shoulder. "I've been thinking about us and our future together."

He hesitated for a split second—and then he grabbed her, jerked her head forward awkwardly, and although he meant to kiss her on the lips, he missed, and swallowed her nose with his mouth.

Bernadine instinctively jumped away, but when he pulled her back, their lips met, and this time they kissed; they kissed as tenderly as Willie could ever imagine kissing or being kissed. Not a short kiss, but a long and lingering one, wet and slippery. Now he knew he had her. He felt her arms snake around his back. She was actually pulling him closer!

Willie had never before felt the tickling, tingling sensation he was feeling right at this moment. He had never seen the stars and stripes and prints of passion that were exploding right before his eyes. He had never been burned by the fire of another person's body. And when she stuck her tongue into his mouth, shoved it right in, painting his teeth with its tip, he had to wrench one hand free, grab onto the cucumber in his crotch, and hold it tight before it exploded.

"Ohhhhh," she sang wetness and warmth into his ear.

"MMMMMMmmmm," he crooned.

This was the most exciting and exhilarating moment of his entire life.

Her arms began to relax a little, but Willie could not bear to let her go. He knew then that if anything was ever going to happen with Willie Heinemann and women, it was going to happen tonight. He knew that if he didn't make his move now, there wouldn't be another time. You have to get a start somewhere and sometime, and already he was five or six years behind the Greenfield kids. Willie was old enough and brave enough. This was it; this was the time. He heard some commotion coming from Middlebaum and Laurel in the kitchen, but everything seemed unimportant and terribly far away right at that moment. His whole future was directly in front of him, within reach. There was no time to worry about other people. Tonight he would show the world what kind of he-man Willie Heinemann really was. The only thing he wanted more than anything was finally within his grasp.

His arm crawled stealthily from around her back and slithered up her stomach. He was coming closer and closer. "I love you," he whispered, "and I want to . . ." He looked longingly over at her bazoongies ". . . touch them."

Immediately, she pulled away. "Willie, no."

But he tried to kiss her and pull her back. "Please."

"No, you can't Willie."

"But I love you." He reached for them, but she knocked his hand away.

"Willie, please stop it."

"I want so very much to touch them. I'll do anything to touch them."

"We've got to go to the party. Don't forget that Rip and Shirley are waiting for us."

"Just one touch. All I'm asking for is a single little touch."

"But Shirley and Rip are waiting. Rip is your friend." She sounded as if she were going to cry. Willie couldn't understand what had gone wrong.

"Don't cry, my darling."

"Please, Willie, please let's go to the party."

He didn't care about the party anymore, or the dugout, or Rip. He didn't even care about Middlebaum dying. His whole body was jumping and shaking, as if he had somehow hooked himself up to an invisible jackhammer. The room whirled around him. The lamp, the chair, the coffee table with the glass top, and the plush orange carpet were spinning. Around and around everything went.

He wasn't asking for much, not much at all. He wasn't asking for the world, he wasn't asking for a million dollars, or a jet plane, or a trip to Tahiti, only a teensy, weensy touch. "I love you," he said.

"No," she stood up and folded her arms over her chest.

He tried to act and speak as calmly and rationally as possible. "You're so beautiful. Your eyes are as blue as buttons, and when you kiss me, I flip."

"Willie, I'm a clean girl. *All I do* is kiss. But unless you stop this right now, I'll never even kiss you again."

He dropped to his knees and wrapped his arms around her ankles in desperation. "Your legs, I love your legs. I love your tongue. I love your lips."

But before anything else could happen between Bernadine and Willie, Laurel came sprinting down the hall, with Middlebaum crawling on his hands and knees in close pursuit.

"They're drunk, Bernie," Laurel cried. "Ronald admitted it. They've been drinking beer all night. And do you know what they planned to do with us down at their hideout?"

"I know, I know, it's terrible! What do they think we are?"

Middlebaum crawled over to Willie, who was still on his knees. "What are you doing down here, Willie?"

"I'm having a private discussion, that's what I'm doing. Now get out of here. Bernadine and I want to be alone."

"No, we don't," Bernadine said.

Middlebaum's tongue was hanging out of the side of his mouth. "I'm sorry, Willie," he said. He leaned over and licked Willie's ear.

"What's wrong with you, Middlebaum? What'd you do that for?"

Middlebaum smiled crazily; his eyes were filled with fog. "Woof!" he said to Willie. "Woof! Woof!"

The urge came into Willie's head so quickly and with such force that he didn't know for sure what was happening. Suddenly his mouth opened and his tongue fell out. "Roaaawwwwaoaooa ruff. Ruff!" he barked.

"Woof-woof-woof," Middlebaum answered. Then he raised his paw and glared up at Bernadine Levine. "Grrrrrrr."

Bernadine must have sensed the danger, for she began backing away. But it was too late. Middlebaum, quick as a whip, sprang from his hind legs, and bit her right on the leg.

For a moment, no one said a word or moved an inch. Willie looked at Middlebaum, and Laurel looked at Willie, and Bernadine looked terrible watching Middlebaum chew on her leg. Then Bernadine screamed, and Laurel yelled, and they both streaked out of the living room with Rin Tin Tin Willie and Ronald Lassie barking and growling after them.

Back into the living room, around the couch, over the coffee table, down the hall, under the kitchen table, over the sink, they all scampered. Up the stairs, the girls screaming and scrambling, the boys bounding and yelping, into the bedrooms, under the beds, around the dressers, past the closets. Middlebaum caught Bernadine's leg two more times. Willie got in a couple of good bites on Laurel's ass. The taste of tender female flesh only whetted their appetites for more.

"Rape, rape, rape," Bernadine and Laurel yelled, as they fled back down the stairs, under the tables and around and around the house. Finally, after a long and exhausting chase, the girls ran into the bathroom, slammed the door, and barricaded themselves inside. Willie and Middlebaum dropped in the hallway, panting.

For a while, Willie stared at the ceiling in silence. Things went blank. There was nothing in front of him except bunkers of coal dust, nothing below him except cool and choppy oceans of India ink. Willie tried walking, swimming, climbing, and crawling, but for a time—perhaps as much as an hour—he could not move, could not see. Was his head pounding? Were the Russians attacking? Or were those bombs bursting really Laurel and Bernadine beating their fists against the bathroom door?

Chapter XIX
Gunfight at the Kiner Corral

"You OK?" Willie asked.

"I don't know," said Middlebaum.

"Neither do I." Willie was sweaty, felt dizzy.

Outside, the air was cool, and the fog in their eyes was partially lifted by the breeze. Peering through the fog and into the sky, Willie could see stars twinkling and twirling like the lights of a faraway ferris wheel.

"You still want to go to the party?" Middlebaum asked.

"Sure, let's go see Rip."

"Fuck Rip," Middlebaum said. "I don't think he made that beer. I think he brought it from home."

"I think Chauncey bought it with Rip's money," said Willie.

"Fuck Chauncey."

"Fuck everybody."

"Fuck those girls," said Middlebaum.

"I never do anything right," said Willie.

"Neither do I. Do you think there's something wrong with us?"

"Well, I have an ulcer."

"I mean something different."

"I know what you mean," said Willie. He looked over at his friend, but couldn't make him out too clearly. The whole world was fuzzy right now. "I don't like to talk about it."

"It just seems that everything is always working out better for other people. It doesn't make sense."

"Nothing makes sense," said Willie.

"Nothing at all."

"Sense doesn't make sense."

"I know what you mean."

"How do you feel?" asked Willie.

"Nothing. I don't feel anything. I know we're walking down the street because I feel us moving, and I see the street, but I'm numb from head to toe."

They managed to navigate the rest of the way down Beechwood Boulevard, up the steps, through the tunnel of bushes and weeds, and stagger into the clearing under the bridge.

"Hey Rip, where the fuck are you?"

"Hey Chauncey?"

"Chauncey, baby?"

"Hey Rip-er-oonie?"

"They might be back with the beer," said Middlebaum. "I'll go see."

Willie's bleary eyes searched the clearing. Potato chips were scattered all around, olives flattened like green pancakes, their bloody pimiento eyes questioning his presence.

"Look what I got," Middlebaum returned, triumphantly holding three bottles of beer in the air.

"I could use a drink," said Willie.

Chauncey's old lantern was still burning a tired blue flame, so they sat around it on the edge of the dugout, dangling their feet inside. They found the opener in the dirt, popped the plugs of the bottles. Middlebaum took the first swig. "Boy, I'm really thirsty. After all we drank, I'm still damn thirsty."

Willie drank, then Middlebaum drank, then Willie drank, then Middlebaum opened another bottle, and they drank some more. Time passed. They talked. What was being said? Willie couldn't remember. He didn't think it really mattered. The whole world was fading.

Willie slid down into the dugout and snuggled up into a corner; the dirt felt cool and soothing on his neck and back. Middlebaum slipped down beside him. Willie was very sleepy. His eyes were closing. He reached over and touched Middlebaum's hand.

Each time Willie opened his eyes, the walls of the dugout spun around him like a lariat, and each time he closed his eyes he felt himself falling. He didn't know where he was falling to, or what he was falling from, but when he closed his eyes, he was suddenly without foundation or gravity, plunging somewhere between time and space and heaven and hell, in the shaft of an elevator without walls or buttons, a hole without an end, a building without a bottom, a ceiling without a floor.

When Willie woke up, he was giggling. He couldn't remember why he was giggling, but he was giggling just the same. Something had been really funny, the funniest thing he had ever heard, and so he laughed and laughed, but he didn't know what was so funny. What the hell was so damn funny? Was it the fact that Middlebaum was dying? "Hey Middlebaum," he said, nudging his friend, "are you dying? You're not dying, are you, you dirty bastard? Nobody dies on Willie Heinemann and gets away with it, I'll tell you that right now."

Willie looked at his friend, the thin frame, the small bony shoulders, the tight, white face. He picked up Middlebaum's head and put it into his lap. He touched Middlebaum's cheeks. There was vomit around the dugout, and vomit on Willie's and Middlebaum's clothes. Willie could smell it, but didn't know who had puked it up. Suddenly, he heard a faraway clatter. No birds were chirping, no crickets were crackling, just the clatter.

CLOPPCLOPPCLOPPCLOPPCLOPP. Willie felt the wind and smelled the dust of the helicopter as it made its descent. He saw God jump out of the cockpit and shake hands with Zeewee who appeared without warning from a cloud of dust and smoke. He saw Zeewee's braves in their bright red warpaint feverishly assembling their cannon, mortar, and machine gun. They were ready almost instantly.

Willie heard Middlebaum whimper in his sleep, first when the cannon went off, KABOOM, and next when the mortar was launched, WHOOSH WOMP, and finally when the machine gun barked, RAT-A-TAT-TAT. A V-2 death rocket droned, then hit nearby, KAPOW. Middlebaum whimpered once more, then fell silent.

What he was seeing and feeling and hearing wasn't really what was happening, Willie knew full well. He knew that God and His helicopter only existed in a make-believe world. Yet, right at this moment, Zeewee, God and His helicopter, and all the things around

Willie that surely did not and could not exist were perfectly real in his mind.

Willie could no longer control his fury. He jumped out of the dugout, pulled a Colt .45 revolver out of his hand-tooled holster, sighting in on Zeewee. Sparks spat from the barrel as the gun barked in his hand. Zeewee fell down dead.

Then Willie stomped across the clearing. He snared God out of the cockpit of His helicopter. He took God's ghostly head and squeezed it into a tight headlock. But God obviously knew judo. He flipped Willie over on his back, picked up a pitchfork, and tried to stab Willie in the face. But Willie moved out of the way, just in time, knocking the pitchfork into the underbrush. Weaponless, God turned and ran. Willie pursued, tackling Him by the ankles. Willie dragged Him through the dirt, picked Him up by the collar, and threw Him against the wall. He slammed God with a left to the chin, a right to the nose, a knee to the belly. Still on His feet, God slumped forward. A rabbit chop from Willie to the back of God's neck thumped God to the ground.

But just as Willie thought he had won the battle, God jumped right back up again. He looked at Willie, smiled slyly, and shook His head from side to side. All the while, He was chuckling. It seemed to Willie that every time he ever came into contact with God, God was smiling or chuckling, making fun and ridiculing one thing or another.

"What's the use, Willie?" God told him. "Don't you see? Ronald Middlebaum was doomed from the very beginning."

* * *

"Willie?" Middlebaum's voice floated into Willie like a dream.
"What?"
"I'm sick."
"I'm sick, too," Willie whispered. "It's the beer. We drank too much," he added.
"No, Willie, I've been sick for a long time."
"You'll be all right."
"No, I won't."
"Sure, you will."

"Willie?"

"What?"

"I might be dying."

Willie felt as if a tree trunk had been dropped inside his stomach, followed by a fireplug and a concrete block. The pain of finally having to face the truth was cold and hard, fiery and numbing simultaneously. For a time, he could not think, could not move, could not, would not, speak or breathe. But he knew that now he had to respond. This time Willie had to deal with himself and his friend. He could not allow himself to remain frozen afraid forever.

"I know about it," he said. "I overheard my parents talking one night."

"So that's why you decided to become my friend." This was not a question.

"Yes."

"Are you glad?"

"Glad I became your friend?"

"Are you?"

"It was pretty good," Willie admitted.

"Willie," Middlebaum said softly, "you think it's true?"

"What's true?"

"That I'm dying?"

Willie thought back nine months to the night he had listened in his bed while his parents had discussed Middlebaum's fate. Willie had been weak and exhausted. He had just been ambushed by his ulcer, and his mother had rescued him from the pain and torture by washing and coddling him. Up to that point in his life, Willie had been attacked and worked over by his ulcer at least once every other week. His mother had always chased the pain away. But now, Willie realized, he hadn't needed his mother's help for a very long time. The ulcer still came and went, but not nearly as often. And Willie had so far been able to endure on his own whatever the ulcer could dish out. Had he set out to save Ronald Middlebaum he wondered? Or had Ronald Middlebaum helped Willie Heinemann save himself?

"Willie," Middlebaum persisted, "you're not answering."

"Answering what?"

"Am I dying, Willie? Do you think so?"

"I guess I do."

The ping pong ball bobbed in the tube of Middlebaum's throat.

"You know, I'll miss you," Middlebaum said into the blue-tinted blackness.

Willie closed his eyes tightly and gritted his teeth.

"You know what I mean, Willie?"

"Yeah Middlebaum, I know what you mean."

Chapter XX

Middlebaum's Last Stand

For weeks after Middlebaum entered the hospital, Willie and Rip and sometimes Chauncey were regularly informed by the nurse at the front desk that their friend wasn't permitted any visitors. The story was always the same. Middlebaum was much too sick to see anybody.

"He doesn't have to see us, we want to see him," Willie explained.

But the nurse didn't know anything about Ronald Middlebaum, and she probably didn't care. "You could always try again tomorrow."

Willie's parents were equally evasive, although Sarah talked faithfully to Ruth Middlebaum each and every day.

"How's Middlebaum doing?" Willie always asked his mother over dinner.

"As well as can be expected."

"What's his mother say?"

"She says he's not eating."

"How does he look?"

"Pale."

"Does the doctor think he'll be all right?"

"Maybe."

"When can I see him?"

"Soon," Sarah would reply.

But despite the attempts of the adult world to cut him off, Willie knew Middlebaum's exact condition because Middlebaum was transmitting regularly on his make-believe walkie-talkie. Over the walkie-talkie, Middlebaum had explained that he was dragged out of his bed the morning after the big party by four men in white coats. He was carried out of the house on a stretcher, inserted into

an ambulance with a whirling red light and a screeching siren, and hauled to the hospital. Then, someone put a mask on his face. From that point on, everything went black. His sheets were black. The food they served him was black. Even the air around him was as black as the black lagoon.

After dinner one night, about a month after Middlebaum's operation, Willie said goodnight to his parents, went into his bedroom, and closed the door. That evening, Middlebaum's signal came in very clearly.

Middlebaum discussed the blackness that had enveloped him since his operation. At first, he could see a faint glimmer of light way out in the distance. It made him feel good. But as time passed, the blackness got thicker. In the beginning, he used his hand to push away the blackness and see the glimmer. Then he needed a spoon, and then a shovel, to see the glimmer of light in the distance. Now, Middlebaum said, he could no longer see, no longer feel, no longer smell anything, no matter how hard he tried. Right now, Middlebaum reported, he could no longer even breathe because of the blackness.

At that very moment, Middlebaum's door was thrown open and his room suddenly exploded in white. It was the white of piano keys, multiplied by the white of angel food, multiplied by the white of pearls and cream and snow and flour and paper and chalk and pigeon-shit and paint, Middlebaum said. There was only one white brighter and whiter than the white that enveloped Middlebaum's room, and that was the object from which all of this white radiated. Middlebaum could see it clearly, as it approached him from the distance.

That was the last time Willie Heinemann had ever heard from Ronald Middlebaum, but before this final transmission went dead, Willie heard the noise. It came from a long way off, sharp and dull at the same time, like the clopp-clopp, thud-thud of a lumberjack's chopping axe.

Lee Gutkind is an Associate Professor in the Department of English at the University of Pittsburgh and Director of the Pitt Writers' Conference.

He is the author of two other books. *Bike Fever* is the story of his odyssey across America on a motorcycle, and *Best Seat in Baseball, But You Have To Stand!* details his adventures on the road with a crew of National League baseball umpires. His documentary film, *A Place Just Right*, featuring the backwoods people of western Pennsylvania, was recently awarded a Golden Eagle by CINE, the Council on International Nontheatrical Events, and selected by CINE to represent the United States in a number of international motion picture events.

Gutkind is also the recipient of a National Endowment of the Arts Creative Writing Fellowship, and has been a fellow at the Virginia Center for the Creative Arts at Sweetbriar. Currently, he is working on a book about the trappers, rattlesnake hunters and other mountain men and women he came to know while making *A Place Just Right*.

Frederick H. Carlson, the illustrator of *God's Helicopter*, is a Connecticut native who moved to Pittsburgh to attend Carnegie-Mellon University in 1973. After graduating in 1977 (with a BFA in Graphic Design), he decided to work as a staff illustrator/designer with the prestigious Pitt Studios. Forming his own studio in 1980, Carlson counts Rockwell International, PPG, US Steel, Westinghouse, Rolling Rock Beer, WQED, and Brockway International among his recent clients. He has exhibited at the Society of Illustrators Gallery in New York (and has a mural in the Museum of Science and Industry in Chicago). Presently, Fred Carlson is a Visiting Artist teaching Illustration to seniors at Carnegie-Mellon. His major outside interest involves playing guitar, mandolin, and banjo. His two immediate goals involve learning how to bow a fiddle and perfecting a system to keep his cats from walking through his palette.

God's Helicopter, in the Slow Loris Press series of books, has been published by Anthony and Patricia Petrosky. Publication of this book was made possible by a grant from the National Endowment for the Arts.